'Wait!' Quick̶ and grasped h

His warm touch had an oddly arresting effect on her.

'Since Dr Geoffrey Hardwick is your father, you must be the sister of Stacey Hardwick?'

Defiantly she met his shrewd gaze, while bowing to the inevitable. What had seemed like a good beginning for herself and Dr Daniels as colleagues was rapidly going down the tubes. She had so wanted him to like her, she realised.

'Yes,' she said, 'of course. And I am very much not like my sister either. For one thing, she's eight years older than I am...we more or less inhabit two different worlds. Emotionally, anyway.'

Still holding her arm, he looked at her so intently, his face not far from hers, that she could not look away. It was as though they were suspended in time and nothing else mattered, as though they were the only two in the world. 'Very glad to hear it, Leila,' he said softly.

Rebecca Lang trained to be a State Registered Nurse in Kent, England, where she was born. Her main focus of interest became operating theatre work, and she gained extensive experience in all types of surgery on both sides of the Atlantic. Now living in Canada, she is married to a Canadian pathologist, and has three children. When not writing, Rebecca enjoys gardening, reading, theatre, exploring new places, and anything to do with the study of people.

Recent titles by the same author:

THE BABY SPECIALIST

BY
REBECCA LANG

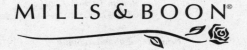
MILLS & BOON®

First published in Great Britain 2003
Harlequin Mills & Boon Limited,
Eton House, 18-24 Paradise Road, Richmond, Surrey TW9 1SR

© Rebecca Lang 2003

ISBN 0 263 83465 4

Set in Times Roman 10½ on 12 pt.
03-0803-51766

Printed and bound in Spain
by Litografía Rosés, S.A., Barcelona

CHAPTER ONE

'THEY'RE doing a Caesarean section in room six, delivering twins, and two people from Social Services have come to take the babies away. You probably saw them in the waiting room.'

Leila Hardwick, RN, nodded as she stood looking down at her supervisor, Donna Parsons, who had delivered this cryptic message. Donna was seated at the desk in her office of the operating suite, known to the staff as the OR for short, at Gresham General Hospital, Ontario.

'Yes, I did see some official-looking people there,' Leila said, exchanging a quick glance with her other colleague, Anne Mackey, who was standing next to her. Anne raised her eyebrows in a meaningful way, saying nothing. They had just arrived together to start the evening shift in the operating suite. It was three-fifteen in the afternoon and they would be there until half past eleven in the evening, at which time the night staff would come on duty.

'May I ask why they're being taken?' she added.

The nursing supervisor rolled her eyes upward. 'Better not to ask too much,' she said dryly. 'The mother can't look after the babies, neither can the father apparently. They're homeless, not in a stable relationship and they're both very young. That's all I know. I'm not sure if the mother wants to keep the babies, but can't.'

'Sounds like Social Services are stepping in for good reasons,' Anne commented.

'Twins are a handful at the best of times,' Leila added, 'without being homeless.'

'I'm sure that Dr Daniels will have a very good reason for getting Social Services in. I'm coming to respect his judgement,' their supervisor went on. 'In fact, he's like a breath of fresh air in this place. He doesn't procrastinate *ad nauseam* like some of the others.'

'Dr Daniels?' Leila said.

'Oh, you haven't met him yet, have you, Leila?'

'No.' She had been away for two weeks, on holiday, when the new staff man on the obstetrics and gynaecology service of the hospital had arrived to take up his post, and she hadn't known his name before she had left. Now the name was jigging an odd memory that she could not place.

'How was your holiday, by the way?' Donna asked, breaking into her train of thought.

'It was good,' Leila said brightly, smiling at the memory. 'Very quiet and restful. I went up to cottage country, to my mother's cabin on Windberry Island, Portage Lake.' She had spent a wonderful two weeks with her mother and sister Stacey on the tiny wooded island in a lake north of Gresham where her mother had a substantial log cabin, painting the pictures from which she made her living. 'It's not often that we manage to have a family gathering.'

'Sounds really good,' Donna said. 'I could use a couple of weeks on an island myself right now. I sure need to get away from this place for a bit. Was your father there?'

'Oh…no,' Leila said. 'It's not often he gets away, even though he's retired now.' Conscious that she was, as usual, making excuses for her father, hearing the false brightness in her own voice, Leila wished that she did not have to do so. Donna Parsons, of all people, knew her father well. After all, she had worked with him for years.

'I bet your mother has something to say about that,' Donna commented as she heaved herself to her feet. A bulky woman, her size betrayed the sedentary nature of her job, tied as she was to her desk most of the time, running the very busy operating suite that dealt with elective surgical cases, as well as emergencies of all types, including the obstetric emergencies.

Leila sighed involuntarily. 'No,' she said, again putting more insouciance into her voice than she felt. 'My mother long ago gave up saying anything, hoping that things could be different. That goes with the nature of his job, I guess. I try to be philosophical about it.'

'Well,' Donna said, 'she isn't the only woman married to a workaholic, and she won't be the last.' She took a set of keys out of the pocket of her white uniform dress. 'Let's check the drugs, girls.'

Anne and Leila smiled at each other behind their supervisor's back as the three of them walked out into the main corridor of the suite and headed towards the drug cupboard that was nearby. When some of the surgeons called them 'girls' it sometimes rankled, but with Donna and the other nursing staff it was something of an 'in' joke.

'Dr Daniels is in room six, doing the section, of course,' Donna said. 'All the paper work for the transfer of the babies has been taken care of, by the way.'

'I'm glad of that,' Anne said. The evening shift could be hectic, without having to do unfamiliar paperwork.

'The mother was on drugs in the recent past,' Donna went on, 'but apparently quit. We're taking no chances with that, and the babies will be transferred to Children's Hospital.' She was referring to the big teaching hospital for sick children in downtown Gresham, not far from Gresham General. 'Apart from that, we have two cases finishing up—an umbilical hernia repair in room four and a gut resection in room two. They're both elective cases. The nurses on ten to six are looking after those. There's nothing else pending, fingers crossed, eh!'

'Sounds OK so far,' Leila said brightly. Again, the name of Dr Daniels nagged at Leila. Where had she heard it before? It was not an unusual name, yet not particularly common either...

'Good,' Anne said. 'I could use a quiet evening.'

Leila looked at her and smiled, thinking ahead to when the other nurses would go home and she and Anne would be on their own until the two night nurses came on duty. They both knew that all hell could break loose between now and then.

When they worked on the day shift, she and Anne usually worked in the gynaecology and obstetrics rooms, two of them, rooms five and six, which were part of the larger operating suite of fifteen rooms. On the evening or night shift it was a different story. They worked in all the specialities, dealing with what ever came in there in the way of emergencies, as well as with any cases that were left over from the operating list of the day, anything that was running late. In that way, they kept their hands in, so to speak, a very necessary constant updating of skills, as all the staff rotated from time to time through those less-than-popular shifts.

When they had checked the drugs, which were kept in a locked cupboard, and the supervisor had gone off duty, Leila and Anne conferred about how they would divide up the work that waited for them.

'I'll take room six, if you like,' Anne said. 'I'm intrigued about Social Services coming to take babies. That doesn't happen very often, does it?'

'No,' Leila said thoughtfully, suspecting that Anne's

eagerness betrayed an interest in the new doctor, as well as in the case.

'We had better find out what the protocol is for that, even though Donna said all the paperwork had been done,' Anne said, 'in case there's a next time.'

'Mmm. Sooner or later there will be a next time,' Leila said. 'It's important to act quickly where babies are concerned, they're so vulnerable.'

'Yes,' Anne said. 'It's better to take action in the very beginning. You read about some awful things in the newspapers.'

'There are so many people these days who want babies, but can't have them,' Leila added.

'Yeah, and adoptive parents are vetted and supervised,' Anne added. 'That's more than you can say for natural parents.'

'You take that room, then,' Leila agreed. 'I'll check on the other cases, let the ''girls'' know we're here, then I'll get a room ready for emergency general surgery as usual. When I've done that, I'll come and help you in room six. Twins are a handful.'

'OK,' Anne said. 'Maybe I'll get a chance to introduce you to Dr Daniels before he leaves for the day. He's rather cute, actually.' She giggled, glancing around her as they stood in the main corridor of the operating suite by the drug cupboard.

'That isn't a word one would normally use for an obstetrician,' Leila said dryly. 'Or any other surgeon, come to that.'

'I know.' Anne grinned. 'In this case, he's not your typical obs and gynae man. For one thing, he does more obstetrics than anything else. He also did training in paediatrics before he decided to do obstetrics. He told me so himself. When he was a medical student he did a lot of volunteer work in some of the poorer countries of South and Middle America. He said he discovered how desperately impoverished women needed obstetric care, and the infant mortality rate is horrendous. The maternal mortality rate probably isn't great either.'

'The same might be said of downtown Gresham sometimes,' Leila said meaningfully. 'You can't force women to go for antenatal care, or take their babies to a doctor or nurse, or stop taking drugs when they're pregnant.'

'He's done downtown Gresham, too,' Anne said. 'That's influenced him for sure.'

'Maybe that's why he decided to go into obstetrics,' Leila mused. 'I'm always curious about why men choose obstetrics.'

'Yeah,' Anne agreed. 'With some, it might be some sort of power trip.'

Leila grinned. 'You could be right there. Dr Daniels must be OK. Not many doctors want to get away from a regular income to go to poor countries or downtown free clinics.'

'Well, he hasn't got a young family to support, not yet, although I've heard he's got at least one serious girlfriend,' Anne said.

'You've discovered a lot in two weeks,' Leila commented, grinning again at her friend's enthusiasm. 'I'm impressed, though I don't see how anyone can have more than one relationship that's serious.'

'I guess he's playing the field a bit,' Anne said airily. 'Anyway, he's just a nice, polite guy.'

'I wonder how long that will last! If he's so cute, as you say, why isn't he married?' Leila commented.

'Search me!' Anne said. 'I expect he's given everything to the job and is just being careful where women are concerned. Better than being divorced.'

'I guess.'

'And another thing.' Anne grasped her friend's arm for emphasis. 'His name's Rupert. His friends call him Rue, apparently, or Rupe.'

'You're kidding.'

'No, I'm not.' Having unburdened herself of that last bit of information, Anne marched off down the corridor and disappeared through the large double doors leading to the subsuite that was the gynaecology and obstetrics unit, leaving Leila standing by the narcotics cupboard staring after her.

'Oh, my God!' Leila whispered the words. 'That's it! Rupert Daniels...Dr Rupert Daniels! I knew there was something familiar about that name. He's here...and I've got to work with him.'

In seconds it all came flooding back then, the memory of how her sister Stacey, eight years her senior, a physiotherapist, had made an utter fool of herself with Dr Rupert Daniels. It was too much to hope for that there would be more than one doctor of that name in this city, that the new one here was someone different, not associated with that fiasco.

Stacey had worked at University Hospital at the time, another big teaching hospital in the city, where Dr Daniels had also worked, where the embarrassing episodes had taken place. Leila's mind flashed over the past events, at the same time as she considered what she had to do now in regard to her immediate duties. It must have been...what? Three years ago? Yes, that must be right, because Stacey had just had her thirty-first birthday then, and had been joking with her family that she was heading for forty.

'There's this gorgeous doctor at the hospital,' Stacey had confided in Leila one weekend when she had come to visit Leila in her small flat in an old converted house near the centre of the city. 'I wouldn't mind asking him to father my baby.'

'What baby?' Leila had said, remembering now the puzzlement she had felt.

'I've made up my mind to have a baby before I'm thirty-five,' Stacey had said casually, almost as though a baby were something that you could order from a shop. 'At least one.'

They had had similar discussions some years before, about whether one could have a baby without being married, whether it would be the right thing for a child, or how difficult it would be to raise a child alone. Theory did not always translate well into practice, Leila had realized as she'd got older.

'All you really need is money and the will to do it, and the love,' Stacey said. 'Look at Mum. She was like an unmarried mother, if ever there was one, raising four children while Dad was working nonstop, as though his life depended on it.'

'She was free to do it, to give us time and attention. And did we like that, not seeing much of him? Did *she* like that?' she said somewhat acidly, while privately agreeing with her sister that having a baby should not depend on being married if you were an independent professional woman, capable of earning the necessary money. Love, time and attention were a different story. 'We *did* have plenty of money. Dad's work saw to that. Would you have that sort of money, Stacey, being on your own?'

'I would do things differently,' Stacey said emphatically, not elaborating on the details.

'How?'

'Oh, I would work part time.'

'Is that where this gorgeous doctor comes in?' Leila

asked sceptically, not really taking her sister seriously. Stacey could be impulsive and unrealistic when she wanted something, though she herself had more common sense.

'Yes,' Stacey said dreamily. 'All I have to do initially is find the right time and place to put the proposition to him.'

'There can't be many men who would want to father a child that they aren't going to have any shared life with,' Leila ventured. 'Or if they don't know that the woman would be a good mother.'

'Are you kidding?' Stacey rounded on her. 'What about all those sperm donors who never see the woman who gets their sperm, let alone see the baby?'

'Those women are often married, the ones who get the donated sperm,' she ventured. 'Their husbands are infertile, and that's a last resort.'

'Plenty are not,' Stacey said impatiently. 'Now there are women who are even donating their ova.'

'Don't do anything stupid.' Leila offered the crude advice, fearing that her sister was a law unto herself and would do exactly as she pleased.

Even so, she did not expect that Stacey would proposition Dr Rupert Daniels—whom she, Leila, had never met—at a hospital party, that she would pursue him relentlessly beyond the point at which a less thick-skinned woman would have retired in gross embarrassment.

In her defence, she was drinking at the party where she first made informal contact with Dr Daniels, so she told Leila afterwards. But after that she pursued him until he told her in no uncertain terms that he wanted nothing to do with her, either professionally or unprofessionally.

Leila cringed again now at the memory. Her sister left University Hospital and took work in the United States.

'Oh, hell,' she muttered to herself now, standing in the empty OR corridor. 'Damn, damn, damn.'

Now she, Leila, must face Dr Rupert Daniels on her own turf, where up to now she had been extremely happy and comfortable. He would have no trouble in associating her with Stacey Hardwick, especially as their father was also at Gresham General. No trouble at all.

Quickly Leila did the rounds of the other rooms that were in use, letting the staff know that the evening shift staff were there, then she began to set up an empty room for all they would need for an emergency of a major general nature, which could be adapted to anything that might come in. Most of the emergencies that they had after regular hours were of an obstetric or gynaecological nature, or orthopaedic cases such as fractured bones, and some of a general nature such as a perforated gut or acute appendicitis.

Then she checked the orthopaedic room, now empty. Road traffic accidents, other than those of a more minor nature, and most other major trauma went to University Hospital, the biggest teaching hospital in the downtown area.

Half an hour later the gut resection case and the hernia case were finished, the patients wheeled out of the respective rooms on stretchers to go to the recovery room. The ten-to-six nurses began to clear up those rooms.

Leila went into room six to check on the Caesarean section. So far, so good, it seemed. The telephone had remained silent with regard to emergencies.

The room was bustling with staff—the surgical team consisting of Dr Daniels and two assistant surgeons, two paediatricians bending over the babies who were in resuscitation carts which kept them warm and administered oxygen to them as necessary, the scrub nurse who was passing the instruments and sutures to the surgeon, and Anne Mackey who was the circulating nurse. The babies were crying lustily, looking perfectly normal to Leila as she took a quick look at them.

'Everything all right here?' she said to Anne, who was busy filling in papers with information about the babies and the surgical procedure.

'Yes.' Anne nodded, looking up, slightly harassed. 'The babies are fine, thank goodness. They cried as soon as they were delivered. The paediatricians are going to hand them over to the social workers, and Dr Daniels is going to talk to the social workers before they go. I'm glad I don't have to do it.'

'They get taken by ambulance to Children's Hospital, isn't that it?' Leila asked quietly.

'Yes, they stay there for a while, get checked out, so I've just discovered,' Anne confirmed. 'We hope they haven't been affected by drugs. That will be also checked out. Then later they go to a foster-home until an adoption can go through. They're going to be kept together.'

'What's the exact story here?' Leila whispered.

'The mother's living on the street, homeless. She's twenty. There is a man who claims that he's the father, but who knows? He's the same age, also homeless,' Anne replied quickly, looking around her to keep a sharp eye on what was going on in the room. 'They're not HIV positive, either of them, thank God.'

'That's something.' Leila shook her head, feeling very sad and sober. There was nothing much to be said, few suitable words. It was not an uncommon scenario. 'All in a day's work, Anne,' she said.

'Yeah.'

Leila glanced at Dr Daniels who was bent forward slightly over his patient on the operating table, his back to her, assisted by his two colleagues. He was tall, slim, broad-shouldered. Dark tendrils of hair curled up slightly from under the back of his operating cap. Leila didn't doubt that he had made the right decision about those babies.

He turned round suddenly and looked at her. Piercing blue eyes looked into hers, and she had the feeling that he had felt her regard. Momentarily she felt mesmerized. So this was the man that Stacey had called 'gorgeous', over whom she had made a fool of herself, unable to help herself, so it had seemed.

'Could someone, please, tell the social workers that we're just about finished here? The babies will be out in a few minutes,' he said to her. 'Tell them not to leave before I've spoken to them. They're going to accompany the babies to Sick Children's.'

Leila nodded, taking note of his low, pleasant voice. 'Right,' she said, her voice sounding to her own ears like a dry croak.

He had a thin, angular face, the bones sharp—the face of an intellectual, she found herself thinking. The eyes were perceptive, coolly appraising. Because of the surgical mask he wore, she could not see his mouth, but could imagine how the remainder of his face would look—very masculine, yet ascetic, without vanity.

There was no spark of recognition in his regard, even though she looked like Stacey in many ways, although not as strikingly attractive, she conceded.

'Could you also check up on the ambulance, make sure it's on its way? It was ordered some time ago, to get here in about ten minutes,' he added.

'Yes,' Leila said, returning his appraisal. Men, she had been told by her women colleagues, were often intimidated by her. With her five-feet-eight height, her apparently cool, sophisticated paleness, her blue eyes, blonde hair, her air of professional competence, she seemed the epitome of efficiency on the job.

Of course, they didn't know how soft she was inside, she thought. No one could tell how much she wanted to pick up the babies and cuddle them, how just looking at them made her feel warmly protective. 'I'll do it now,' she said.

'Thanks.' He turned back to the job in hand.

'Ready for closure,' the scrub nurse said to Anne. 'Ready for the sponge and instrument count.'

Leila left the room, going to an external telephone just outside to call the ambulance service to check that the ambulance was on its way.

'Phew!' She let out a pent-up breath, suddenly aware that she had been holding herself stiffly. So that was the gorgeous Dr Daniels. She had got over the first hurdle of meeting him...sort of. Now she had time to build up her defences for the inevitable moment when the light would dawn in his eyes when he heard her name. Maybe he had put Stacey to the back of his mind in the ensuing three years, or on the other hand he might have been overly sensitized to potential problems with female colleagues to the point where he was merely bland and polite, confining all conversation to work issues.

Either way, she would soon find out.

CHAPTER TWO

THE two social workers, both women, were waiting in a small sitting area for visitors just inside the main entrance to the operating suite.

'The babies will be out in a few minutes,' Leila said. 'Dr Daniels wants to speak to you before you take them, and I've confirmed that the ambulance is on its way—should be here in less than ten minutes.'

'How are the babies?' one of them asked.

'As far as I can tell, they look good. They're both a good size, and certainly making a lot of healthy noise,' Leila said, smiling.

Both women smiled back. One was middle-aged, obviously well experienced, while the other one was younger. 'That's a relief,' the older one said. 'We thought they might be brain-damaged because of the drugs. Of course, it's too early to tell for sure really.'

'What will happen to them?' Leila asked. 'They look like lovely babies. Will they be adopted together?'

'Yes. We have a family all lined up to take them. We're going to keep them in hospital for a while to do some tests, make sure they're all right, then they'll stay in a foster-home under our supervision for a while, during which time the adoptive family will get to know them and handle them, then they'll gradually ease into the adoptive family. We'll be in the picture ourselves for quite some time.'

'Taking on twins is quite a job,' Leila commented, thinking of the babies and how she would manage herself if she had them, 'without having a possible drug-withdrawal problem as well.'

'That will be dealt with before we let them go,' the more mature social worker said. 'We're hoping it's not going to be anything permanent. The adoptive family has one child of their own already, so they are experienced parents.'

'Will the mother get to see them?'

'No. She didn't want to. She thought it best, and we agreed, under the circumstances. It's not that she doesn't care,' the social worker said thoughtfully, 'but she thinks that letting them go might upset her more if she's seen them first. But she did say that she wants to maintain some sort of contact with them, and maybe see them when they're older.'

'Maybe just as well,' Leila said soberly, feeling a deep sadness. Inevitably, she imagined herself with those lovely babies, picturing how she would cope. 'Well, they'll be out in about five minutes.'

When Leila went back into room six the sponge and instrument count had been done, the closing-up procedure started. Dr Daniels was just 'scrubbing out', stripping off his soiled surgical gown and latex gloves, leaving his assistants to finish suturing up the patient's abdomen.

'And who are you?' he asked, coming over to Leila, who happened to be standing by the laundry bin as he flung his gown into it. 'I don't think we've met.'

His eyes went over her quickly, from her head down to her feet and back again, a common enough gesture in the OR where attractions could be rampant if not held in check among members of the large team that worked there. She prided herself on being very professional. Yet, to her annoyance, she felt her heart give a rare flip of awareness, signalling a reluctant attraction. The last thing she wanted was to repeat any of her sister's behaviour, she told herself fiercely as her cheeks flushed behind the covering face mask.

At least he wasn't one of those arrogant types who dropped his soiled clothes on the floor for someone else to pick up. There were already enough of that ilk, she thought wryly. That was something.

She cleared her throat. 'I'm Leila Hardwick, RN,' she said.

He held out a hand. 'Rupert Daniels,' he said, gripping her tentative hand firmly. 'How come I haven't seen you before?'

'I was on holiday for two weeks,' she said, aware that her voice was stiff, her eyes searching his face swiftly for any sign of recognition. There was none. 'This is my first day back.'

'Ah, that explains it,' he said, his eyes smiling at her over his surgical mask.

She always preferred to maintain a professional relationship with the doctors in the operating suite, especially the obstetricians with whom she had to work closely. With this man she was already feeling an unusual sense of curiosity, with something approaching dread at the possible awkwardness that might ensue when he knew that she was Stacey's sister.

'Normally I work in this service for the day shift,' she added. And another thing, she told herself, this man was informal without being familiar, with an understated charm that left her feeling uncharacteristically vulnerable to his good looks. She was beginning to see what Stacey had meant. Not for him the innuendo or snide hints where attraction was concerned. She sensed that he would be very good at his job, very professional, while being personable, calm, and naturally polite and empathetic. After a few years of working in the OR one's intuition about colleagues was seldom wrong.

'In that case,' he said, 'I look forward to working with you.'

Leila smiled slightly, wondering whether she should return the compliment, then deciding not to in case it sounded too familiar. 'Oh?' she found herself saying, trying to be flippant because she was somehow disarmed by him. 'I usually prefer to reserve judgement, myself, until I know something of the nature of the beast.'

To her surprise, he laughed. 'I usually find most nurses agreeable,' he said. 'I've recently come from University Hospital, and I expect to find the nurses just as good here.'

'I expect they are,' she said. 'I've told the social workers you are on your way out to talk to them, and the ambulance will most likely be here by now.'

'Great. Thanks,' he said. 'Could you help bring the babies out? I want to have them out of the room before the mother comes round from the anaesthetic.'

'Did she really not want to see them?' Leila blurted out.

'Yes. She has her reasons.'

'It's so…sad,' she said, feeling the inadequacy of the word.

'Yes, it is. But that's also fine, as at least they have a good home to go to.'

'Yes, I expect they'll have a good life,' she agreed, forcing her thoughts ahead to the family that was waiting for those babies, while the babies themselves were both quiet in their incubators.

'If you were in that situation, what would you do, Leila Hardwick? I'm always curious about different views, bearing in mind the old expression that it takes all sorts to make a world.' He looked at her astutely, his blue eyes unforgiving in their intensity. It would be very difficult to lie to this man.

'Oh, I don't suppose I would give them up,' she said quickly, glancing sideways again at the babies. 'I don't think I could bring myself to do it.'

'Not even if you were twenty and homeless?' he asked, still looking at her keenly, a cynicism in his expression.

'I don't think so. How could I part with my own flesh and blood?' she said. 'But the young are subjected to all sorts of pressures to behave in a certain way…apart from the practicalities of the situation. It's easy to judge others, isn't it? When you haven't been in the situation yourself.'

'Yes. You seem very forgiving, Ms Hardwick,' he said.

'There's an old saying that circumstances alter cases,' she said. 'I've never known what it is to be homeless, to lack money or be addicted to drugs. Even so, I can't imagine giving up a baby.'

'You do something to restore my faith in human nature,' he said, smiling slightly. 'Excuse me. Nice to have met you.' Quickly he left the room.

'Are the babies ready to be moved out, Dr Nin?' Leila asked one of the paediatricians, Dr Clara Nin, with whom she worked frequently and liked very much for both her warm personality and her professional competence.

'Hello, Leila. Welcome back,' Dr Nin smiled at her. 'Yes, they're ready now. What do you think of our new obs and gynae man?'

'Well, he seems like a good surgeon as far as I can tell so far. And he seems very…nice,' she said carefully.

'Yes, he is nice.' Dr Nin smiled at her. 'We were in the same class at medical school.' To Leila there seemed to be undercurrents in Dr Nin's remarks, a subtlety that Leila did not have time to fathom at that moment. There was just time for her to register certain nuances in the other woman's words.

'Would you like to take one of the babies?' Dr Nin asked. 'I'll take the other.'

'Yes. A boy and a girl?' Leila asked, looking at the babies swaddled in flannelette blankets, one blue, one pink.

'Yes, and beautiful babies, too, considering,' Dr Nin said as she expertly picked up the pink bundle from the resuscitation cart, cradled it in the crook of an arm, then picked up a sheaf of papers with her free hand. 'Come on, let's get them out of here. The sooner they get to Sick Children's the better, although they seem fine to me.'

Leila stepped forward and picked up the blue bundle, feeling as she did so a familiar warm sense of protectiveness for the tiny scrap of humanity. A lot of newborn babies looked as though they had come through an ordeal, which, in fact, they had, with an expression on their faces as though they had all the cares in the world. This particular baby, she thought tenderly as she looked down at the scrunched-up face with the wisp of dark hair falling forward over his forehead, had had the cards stacked against him—together with his sister—more than most. Help had come to reverse the tide of unfortunate circumstances in the shape of Dr Rupert Daniels. She assumed he had been the one who had initiated all this, had started them on the path that should turn out well for them.

Of course, by working in the OR, they only saw the pregnant women who had difficult deliveries, the women who needed Caesarean sections. They did not see the normal deliveries which took place in the labour ward. Social circumstances could be difficult also for those women who had the so-called normal deliveries. There were women who longed for babies, and those at the other end of the spectrum who had to give up their babies.

Dr Daniels was with the social workers, conferring with them. Leila could see him properly now as his surgical mask dangled around his neck and revealed a face much as she had imagined it—a square-cut jaw, a determined chin and a very masculine mouth that was now stretched in a smile as he saw the babies.

'Ah,' he said, holding out his arms to Leila to take the baby she was holding. His hands brushed warmly and gently against her arms as they made the transfer, again making her uncharacteristically aware of him, and she found herself recoiling. It was a sensation that made her angry with herself. The thought flashed through her mind that perhaps she was getting to a stage in her life where she needed a permanent relationship, and she didn't have one... Work had taken over her life just lately.

More and more, now that she was in her mid-twenties, she thought of the baby that she would like to have. Looking at the very attractive Dr Daniels, her mind quickly shied away from that. For the first time, she understood instinctively something of what Stacey had felt at the age of thirty-one...

'Thank you, Leila,' he murmured to her.

There was no way that she wanted to be more than ordinarily aware of the men she worked with—that tended to bring little but trouble in the already heightened atmosphere of the operating suite, where the staff worked in close proximity. Her resolve not to get involved with a doctor was proving difficult to maintain when most of the men she met were in the medical profession.

Leila hovered for a few moments to see what was to happen next. Two ambulancemen came in with special containers for the babies, and it was established that Dr

Nin would accompany the two social workers to the Children's Hospital.

'Cheer up, Leila,' Dr Nin said, looking at her perceptively. 'These babies are going to have a great life. I know the family they're going to.'

'I hope so,' Leila said, feeling her face flush as all eyes were momentarily on her. Indeed, she had felt a sadness at handing over the warm bundle, a sadness at the utter vulnerability of that little scrap of humanity whose biological mother and father were not able to take care of him or his sister.

She saw Rupert Daniels look at her speculatively, his eyebrows raised in a questioning way. Maybe he was wondering if she thought that the babies should have been left with their mother, no matter what. Quickly she looked at him and away again.

'It's better this way,' he said quietly to her, having come to stand beside her now that the babies were out of his hands, his voice lost to others in the general bustle of activity as they prepared to depart. His proximity was making her feel vulnerable again, peculiarly touched by him singling her out for a few seconds of extra commiseration.

Leila nodded.

'Also,' he added, 'by doing it this way, several people outside the adoptive family will be keeping close tabs on the babies. That's very important, and the natural mother will be able to keep in contact if she wishes.'

Again she nodded, wondering at the muted fierceness in him, wondering what cases he had encountered in his career that had hardened his determination in that direction. There seemed to be a bitterness in him, her intuition told her, and she wondered if it had anything to do with Stacey. No, she decided. Stacey would most likely have been a good mother, would have wanted her baby very much.

The group of people left, going through the wide double doors of the operating suite, leaving her alone with Dr Daniels. As he turned to her again, as though he would say something more, Leila stepped back with a muttered, 'Excuse me.'

She moved away from him, not knowing what else to say, and, turning quickly on her heel, walked from him down the corridor. Those babies, she told herself, were going to have a good life. Nonetheless, she felt oddly emotional. Tears pricked her eyes, which perhaps came from dredging up all the old memories about Stacey and her peculiar would-be relationship with Rupert Daniels. Nothing had really come of it. During her recent holiday with her mother and sister, there had been no mention of babies, or of Rupert Daniels.

Back in room six she helped Anne and the anaesthetist to supervise the transfer of the young woman patient onto a stretcher, on which she would be taken to the recovery room, the woman who looked like a girl of about fifteen rather than twenty. She had a thin, very pale face and untidy hair escaping from the blue paper cap that was supposed to cover it, which made her look very vulnerable.

'It looks as though she needs a mother herself,' Leila commented in a whisper, feeling an empathy with this woman, 'instead of being one.'

'Yes,' the anaesthetist agreed softly, so that their patient, who was coming round from the anaesthetic, would not hear. 'Most of these girls have not had adequate mothering themselves, not enough of anything good or stable in their lives. Maybe this girl knew what she was about when she decided to give up her own babies.'

'Yeah, what do we really know about it?' Anne commented.

'Wake up, Cathy,' the anaesthetist said to the young woman, tapping her cheek gently with his hand, bending down to her. 'Open your eyes. The operation's over. Everything's fine.'

Groggily the patient opened her eyes and stared unseeingly at the ceiling and the bright lights.

'I want you to take some deep breaths,' the anaesthetist said as he held an oxygen mask over her nose and mouth while Leila and Anne stood by. 'The oxygen will help you breathe easier.'

Then they all helped to push the stretcher to the recovery room. As Leila left their patient in the capable hands of one of the recovery room nurses, she vowed that she would try to find time to speak to the young mother before she was transferred to an obstetrics floor.

'Maybe she'll regret it later in her life, but right now that's her only option,' Anne commented as they walked back along the corridor to face the mess the operation had created in room six. When they had cleared and cleaned the room, it would have to be set up for another case as soon as possible.

'I know this is a cliché,' Anne said, with the air of one dealing a prophetic judgement, 'but this is a funny old world, isn't it?'

'Sure is, Anne,' she said. 'It's easy to judge, isn't it, when you have a good home yourself?'

'You said it.'

'Meanwhile, on with the fray.' Leila began to swab down the black rubber top of the operating table with surgical spirit to clean it, thinking that most people took good things for granted, until they were no longer available.

'What about us? We're both twenty-six,' Anne suddenly blurted out. 'Are you going to wait until you're thirty-six to have a baby?'

'I don't know,' Leila said, working furiously, glancing at the wall clock. 'It's something I think about quite a lot, but not something I want to go into right now, Anne.' No, the combination of meeting Rupert Daniels, thinking about Stacey and seeing the twins, who might never get to know their real mother, left her tense. 'Let's just say that it worries me at times. When I was holding that baby just now I wanted him for myself.'

She hadn't told Anne about her sister, who was now thirty-four and still childless and unmarried. Pensively, she wondered whether she should tell her. Maybe she would wait to see if Dr Daniels drew the obvious conclusion that she was related to Stacey. Maybe for him the whole issue had not been so fraught; maybe he had dismissed it as another occupational hazard. Well, she for one was not going to let him know that she found him attractive if she could possibly help it, was not going to add anything to his ego, which must already be pretty inflated. Imagine being pursued as a stud, she thought.

'Personally, I'm going to have a baby when I'm thirty, married or not,' Anne said decisively.

Leila declined to answer with a revelation of her own.

'Would Rory make a good father, do you think?' Anne asked somewhat archly, referring to Leila's friend with whom she sometimes played tennis, a physiotherapist at the hospital.

The image of Rory, who had been introduced to her by Stacey, entered Leila's mind. They hadn't seen each other since she had returned from her holiday. 'I haven't thought about him in connection with fatherhood,' Leila said honestly, as she shook out a green cotton sheet to cover the operating table in readiness for their next patient, whoever she might be. 'He's just a friend.'

'Do you love him?'

'Of course not!' she said. 'I don't really know what love is, but I do know what it's not, Anne. I'm hoping for something tempestuous.'

'Don't we all?' Anne said, laughing, as she aimed a bundle of disposable drapes into a plastic bin.

'I just don't want to marry a doctor,' Leila added. She and Anne had had an ongoing discussion about the dilemmas of life over the years that they had known each other in their shared training and education in the nursing school at the university in Gresham.

Anne, quickly and automatically, began setting up the anaesthetic cart with clean equipment for the next case.

'There don't appear too many great guys around who would make good fathers,' Leila said pensively.

'Right.'

When Leila saw Anne's eyes move from her to look towards a partially open side door to the room, leading to the area of the scrub sinks where surgeons frequently stood to write up their post-operation notes, she turned round. Dr Daniels was standing in the half-open door silently looking at them. How long he had been there she had no idea. He had a pen in his hand and a sheaf of papers. There was a slightly amused quirk to his mouth and a certain light in his eyes.

'Oh, heck!' Leila muttered to herself. He must have heard every word they had said over the past few minutes.

CHAPTER THREE

'I SEEM to be interrupting a philosophical conversation,' Dr Daniels said, that speculative smile deepening on his face as he looked from one to the other and came farther into the room. That smile said it all.

Against her will, and to her deep mortification, Leila found herself blushing with embarrassment. As far as she could see, there was still no look of recognition on his face.

'Oh, this is something we do all the time. We've done it for years,' Anne said airily. 'You know how it is—a lot of theory, untested by even one scrap of practical evidence.'

'I see,' he murmured. 'Um…I just wanted to remind you that I'm the staff man on call for the remainder of this evening for obs and gynàe—and for the night also.'

'Yes, we did know, thank you, Dr Daniels,' Anne said demurely, giving him one of her most charming smiles.

Rupert Daniels looked from one to the other. 'Just page me if you need me. I'll be either in the hospital or very close to it,' he said.

Leila swallowed, very conscious of her heated face and his very discerning stare, the light of amusement still in his eyes. 'All right,' she said. 'Er…is there anything pending that you know of?'

'No. I haven't any women in labour at the moment. And there's nothing in Emergency. I just checked,' he said, holding her gaze.

'Good,' she said, striving for a professional note.

'Thank you both, and I hope it will be "goodnight",' he said.

'I won't say "goodnight" because that will jinx us for sure,' Anne said. 'See you later, Dr Daniels.'

He looked at them both. Just then a telephone outside the room rang shrilly, and Anne went out to answer it, leaving Leila feeling trapped.

'That desire for something "tempestuous" will be quite a challenge to someone, Ms Hardwick,' he said, now grinning openly.

'Yes, it will be,' she said, her face flaming anew. 'When I find it, I expect I shall be quite up to dealing with it.'

With that, he laughed openly, the amusement transforming his face from attractive to devastating. 'Good hunting,' he said.

Leila swallowed nervously.

'Well, goodnight,' he said, backing out of the room.

'Goodnight.'

His footsteps echoed down the corridor.

'That was the blood bank,' Anne said, rushing back into the room. 'They wanted to know the whereabouts of the gut resection patient.'

Not a new case, then. Leila relaxed a bit. 'Do you think he heard everything we said?' she whispered.

'I expect so,' Anne said, finishing up her work. 'He had that sort of knowing look on his face, while trying not to show it.'

'Damn!'

'Not to worry,' Anne said.

'I'll go and get the packs for emergencies,' Leila said, grabbing the small instrument trolley to take to the stockroom to get several of the very large sterile packs of linens and disposable drapes for patients, plus the Caesarean instrument trays which contained all the equipment that they would need for an emergency operation in that room.

'OK,' Anne said. 'I'll finish up here and set up the baby-resuscitation cart, then we're all ready here.'

On the way to the stockroom Leila looked in on the other two rooms where the elective cases for the day had been finished up, to find that the ten-to-six nurses had finished clearing those rooms and were well on the way to setting them up again for whatever might be needed for the unexpected.

'So far, so good.' She breathed the words again to herself. She was the nurse in charge for the evening shift. It was up to her to ensure that the unit was in a state of perfect readiness for whatever might come their way and to make sure that everything went smoothly and efficiently. It was the night nurses who would do most of the setting-up for the routine operating list for the following day, although the evening nurses did as much as they had time for.

Leaving her wheeled cart in the stockroom, she decided to take this opportunity to talk to Cathy, the young mother, before she was transferred to the post-op obstetrics floor. If she did not take advantage of this slight lull, she might not get another chance. Once the young woman was back on the floor, she might clam up as far as discussing her situation was concerned—right now she might be more open to some commiseration. Somehow it seemed imperative to Leila that she find out whether the mother had voluntarily given up her children.

'Hello, Cathy,' she said, bending near the pale face of the girl who lay on the stretcher. 'I'm one of the nurses who was there when you had your operation.'

An intravenous line of clear plastic carried fluid into a vein in the back of Cathy's hand, while a vaporizer moistened oxygen that was being given to her via tubes in her nose. An automatic blood-pressure cuff, wrapped around her upper arm, inflated and deflated noisily, while the re- sult appeared on a monitor screen, together with the pulse rate, body temperature and level of circulating oxygen.

'I wanted you to know that the babies are all right,' she said gently, 'although I expect that Dr Daniels has spoken to you already.'

'Yes,' the girl whispered, nodding wearily. The skin of her face was so pale that it looked almost translucent, her eyelids a bluish colour. She appeared fragile, like a fine porcelain doll that might break. Likewise, her hands were small, almost like the hands of a child.

Still under the influence of the painkilling drugs she had been given, Cathy looked up without guile. 'I'm glad they're all right,' she said. 'I do love them, you know...I loved them when I felt them moving about inside my body. But I can't look after them. It's no good pretending that I can.' Although she was matter-of-fact, Leila sensed the deep emotion behind her words, and she herself felt her throat close up with emotion.

'Yes, I understand,' Leila said gently.

'I might have kept one,' the girl went on, 'but I couldn't cope with two. And I wanted them to be together, you see. That way, at least they'll have each other...'

'Yes. They're lovely babies...beautiful,' Leila said.

At that, the girl began to cry softly, the tears rolling down her cheeks. It would have been easy, and fatuous, for Leila to have said that everything was all right, when clearly it was not all right for this young woman, so she refrained from doing so.

'They're getting a lot of good attention,' she said. 'And I've heard that they're going to a loving home.'

Again Cathy nodded dumbly, her misery palpable. 'I'll

see them at some point,' she said, 'when I don't feel so emotional. Is Dr Daniels coming to see me again? I would like to see him.'

'Oh, yes, I expect he will,' Leila said. 'You'll see a lot of him before you get to go home.'

'He helped me to keep going,' the girl said simply. 'I had to give them up. I didn't have a real choice. I've got no one to help me, you see…' Cathy's voice trailed off.

'Yes. Everyone understands, Cathy,' Leila said gently, struck by how vulnerable a human being this girl really was.

As though on cue, they heard Rupert Daniels's voice nearby, and Leila turned to see him coming towards them. 'Here's Dr Daniels,' she said, touching Cathy's hand briefly, 'come to see you. I've got to go now. You take care.'

Cathy's face lit up as she looked beyond Leila to Rupert Daniels. As Leila left the scene, her colleague smiled at her as they passed.

In the stockroom she took her time to sort through and pile the selected packs and trays of instruments onto her wheeled table, her emotions very close to the surface. In this place you often saw the raw side of life. You saw people at their most vulnerable, sometimes desperate, having to face intolerable dilemmas.

Just as she was about to leave, there were, abruptly, voices out in the corridor, as though two people had walked down it swiftly and stopped nearby. One voice was all too familiar to her—her father's. The other she recognized also, belonging to Dr Rupert Daniels.

'What possessed you to take those babies away from the family?' her father's irascible voice demanded, at which Leila cringed. 'I made it my policy to keep families together at all costs.'

'At all costs to the baby?' Dr Daniels said. 'In this case, it's two babies.' It was clear to Leila that he was angry, and she stood quietly, holding her breath, waiting for a retaliatory outburst from the other man. 'In this case, there *is* only the mother and she's in no position to cope alone.'

'You have to give them a chance to make a family,' the other man said.

'With all due respect, are you kidding?' Rupert Daniels said. 'There's no home, both parents are on the street. They're both young, poorly educated, no job training or experience to speak of, no way of earning money and both on hard drugs until very recently.'

'You have to give them a chance. Give them time,' the other man said.

There was a silence which Leila, daring now to breathe shallowly, interpreted as fraught and exasperated. The incredulity of the younger man was evident in that silence.

'Time is what we don't have,' she heard Dr Daniels say after a moment or two. 'You can't dice with children's lives.'

'Point taken,' the other said. 'When I was Head of Department I would simply have kept the mother in hospital longer, to keep an eye on her and the babies.'

'And if she refused?' came the exasperated retort. 'Perhaps, Dr Hardwick, it's just as well that you are no longer Head of Department. Let me tell you now that a very important part of my mandate here is to protect those who cannot protect themselves—the babies that I deliver. I will never discharge a baby into a dangerous situation. I will also do what I can to protect the child-mothers.'

The reply was swift, hectoring. 'I still maintain that you have to give them a chance. If I have anything to do with it, you won't be continuing those tactics for very long. You're young and inexperienced.'

'I'm not exactly young, Dr Hardwick,' Rupert Daniels said. 'And I've seen enough of the world…and not just in Gresham, Ontario,' he added pointedly, 'to be able to recognize a potentially dangerous situation when I see one. I prefer prevention, rather than trying to patch up a bad situation after the fact.'

'You exaggerate,' came the familiar arrogant reply, scathing in tone, at which Leila felt her face flush with embarrassment and an inward cringing.

'I doubt, Dr Hardwick, that you will have anything to do with it,' Rupert Daniels replied tersely. 'And having been retired for two years, I do not think you have a right to dictate policy to the department. You are here because you still have patients who want to see you, not to influence the running of the department.'

'We'll see about that.'

'As for those babies,' Rupert Daniels went on, 'someone has to be accountable. If not me, who?'

The older man said nothing.

Leila held her breath again in astonishment. No one, as far as she knew, had ever had the nerve to speak to Geoffrey Hardwick in that forthright manner, telling him a few home truths which he, no doubt, did not want to face up to.

At that moment the piercing note of a pager interrupted the dialogue, and she heard footsteps retreating. Letting out a pent-up breath, she pushed her trolley out into the corridor.

It was Dr Daniels outside, leaning against the wall, rather than her father whom she had been expecting.

'Oh,' she said, her flush deepening, while he stared at her from a face that was a shade paler than when she had last seen it, his eyes angry.

'Leila Hardwick,' he said after a moment. 'I guess the

shoe is on the other foot now, eh? You've been unwittingly listening to my conversation with the former head of the obs and gynae department.'

He stood up straight, frowning at her as a slow realization seemed to dawn on his face. It was what she had been dreading. 'Are you…er…by any chance related to him—Dr Geoffrey Hardwick?' he asked softly, his gaze intent, his eyes seeming to bore into her.

Leila cleared her throat. 'Um…yes,' she said soberly. 'He's my father.'

The short silence that followed was uncomfortable as he regarded her. 'Like father, like daughter?' he queried, frowning down at her with what she interpreted as a cynical expression on his face.

'No, not at all,' she said, shaking her head for emphasis. If only he knew how far away from her father's philosophy she was, and had always been, how that resistance had coloured her whole life, he would not have asked that question. Yet, perversely, she knew that her father had a right to his professional and personal opinions. 'I'm afraid he can't seem to forget that he's no longer Head of Department, or remember that he's past retirement age.'

'A pity,' he said.

The comment sparked unexpected anger in Leila as in her heightened emotional mood she thought she detected a sarcasm in his tone. 'He is not incompetent,' she said emphatically, 'in any way. Even so, I feel that I must apologize for him.'

Almost against her will she felt a sense of protectiveness and empathy towards her father, who was, she knew, well able to protect himself in most ways, although the reality of his retirement was something that he didn't seem able to accept yet. 'He's always been very good at his job,' she stated defensively, 'and I believe he still has something to offer this hospital and the university. Others seem to think so, anyway. And, Dr Daniels, he does have a right to his opinion, even though it differs from yours.'

Her cheeks were red now, feeling as though they were on fire. He shouldn't have been sarcastic, she told herself. After all, he had scarcely been in the place for five minutes. 'He's been here a long time,' she added. 'He's devoted several decades to the place.'

'I do understand that,' he said, looking at her speculatively, taking in her flushed face with what seemed to her a detached interest.

'He's like a lot of doctors,' she went on hotly. 'He's made his career his whole life. Maybe it was inevitable in his generation. It's a common phenomenon.'

Not sure why she was defending her father when it was her mother with whom she was in sympathy, she nonetheless found herself driven to do it in the face of this young doctor. It was her mother who had endured a lonely married life, almost like an unmarried mother, while her father had devoted himself to his career. Her mother had run the household like a well-oiled machine, had raised and loved three children, trying to give them enough love for two parents to make up for the almost always absent father.

Somehow, in a perverse way, Leila's anger at her father was transferring itself to this doctor before her, one who had chosen the same career. While she vaguely recognized what was happening, she had rushed on regardless.

'I'm trying to understand that, too, which, as you say, is common enough.' Dr Daniels said while she was gathering her thoughts for further verbal defence. 'I can't say that I ascribe to that practice, although I know too well how it happens. Are you saying that I should overlook his remarks?' Again, it seemed to her, there was a note of mild sarcasm in his voice.

'No. Please, don't think I condone what he says. We…we don't always agree on things, I…I'm sad to say. But he *is* my father…' Leila let her voice trail off as she was unable to sustain eye contact with the very perceptive Rupert Daniels.

'As you say, he has a right to his views. But he's no longer officially on staff, even though he sees patients here. He's not allowed to operate any more, as you know. He'll probably report me to the current head,' Dr Daniels said, 'for what he would see as insubordination. Maybe he thinks I'm still a resident instead of a staff man.'

'I don't think Dr Smythe would take a lot of notice,' Leila said, referring to the current head. 'He's a very reasonable man.'

'Maybe not. It just creates an uncomfortable and unnecessary atmosphere, that's all,' he said. 'I believe that what I arranged for those twins was the right thing. There was no other possibility. Perhaps your father tends to deny the unpalatable realities of this city.' The look he gave her was perceptive and, it seemed to her, challenging.

'Perhaps he does,' she admitted. 'He has a different approach, more paternalistic, and maybe he is a bit out of touch with the drug culture, the way things have changed in recent years.'

Thoughts of her mother flooded over Leila again, of the lonely years that she had endured. The holiday they had recently shared on Windberry Island had brought those years back forcefully as, for the first time in a long time, Leila had seen her mother happy because she had met fellow artists who had recently bought cabins on the island. Their shared interests had suddenly brought her mother to life in a different way. For once there were other adults, both men and women, to listen to her, who shared her love of art, who found her interesting.

Memories of her mother's happiness as she had encountered the unexpected companionship and compatibility with fellow artists brought the sting of tears to Leila's eyes now, tears of regret for lost years. Until that moment she hadn't realized how close to the surface her emotions were with regard to her parents now that her father was suffering, too, because of his retirement. Her father, who had provided plenty of money for his family from his hard work, had seldom performed the role of a loving, supportive spouse or companion. It had been difficult for her mother to complain when their material needs as a family had been taken care of so well. That support had been left to her children and close friends.

'Hey,' Dr Daniels said, leaning forward to look at her closely, 'I haven't upset you, have I?' Unexpectedly, he put a finger under her chin and lifted her face up as he peered down at her with concern. His touch was warm and oddly shocking, as she had not expected it. In a moment he released her. 'I didn't mean to.'

'No, nothing to do with that,' Leila said, blinking back the moisture in her eyes, forced to meet his scrutiny. Embarrassed, she blurted out what was on her mind. 'Your comments made me think about how my father has never really contributed as much as he could have done to family life. The job always took priority. It's…it's so incongruous really, that he should take the stance that he takes—going on about the family as though it was somehow sacred. But I guess he saw his contribution as material.'

Already she had said more than she had intended to this man who was little more than a stranger. Perhaps she would regret her confidence when they had to work closely together in the future.

Rupert Daniels nodded. 'That's part of the overwork syndrome,' he said. 'Thinking that material things can make up for time, attention and affection freely given.'

So he did understand. 'Sounds simple, doesn't it? But it's not,' she said.

'No, it isn't. Is that why you have the views that you do about marriage?' he suddenly asked, taking her unawares, letting her know that he had overheard the conversation she had had with Anne.

'Well…yes, I suppose that is why,' she admitted.

'Such strong views for such a mundane reason,' he murmured.

'It may sound mundane to you,' she said, annoyed, 'but it's not when you've grown up with the consequences every day of your life.'

'I do understand,' he said. 'But surely you don't need to order your whole life on what your parents have done— if you'll forgive me for being personal.'

'Perhaps not, but at the moment I don't know any other way. I…must go,' she said abruptly. 'Excuse me.' She pushed the trolley past him. 'I've got work to do.'

'Wait!' Quickly he reached out and grasped her arm, which was bare below the short sleeve of the scrub-suit top. His warm touch had an oddly arresting effect on her. 'Since he's your father, you must be the sister of Stacey Hardwick?'

Defiantly she met his shrewd regard, bowing to the inevitable. What had seemed like a good beginning for Dr Daniels and herself as colleagues was rapidly going down the tubes, she thought rather desperately. She had so wanted him to like her, she realized now, to find out that she was not like Stacey.

'Yes,' she said, 'of course. And I am very much *not* like my sister either. For one thing, she's eight years older than I am, and we more or less inhabit two different worlds. Emotionally, anyway.'

Still holding her arm, he looked at her so intently, his face not far from hers, that she could not look away. It was as though they were suspended in time and nothing else mattered, that they were the only two in the world. 'Very glad to hear it, Leila,' he said softly.

'Um…' she began, not sure what she was going to say, trying to ad lib.

'I shall keep you to that—a promise not to be the same,' he said, still speaking softly, reflectively, as though she were a phenomenon that he couldn't quite fathom, 'since we have to work together. One like Stacey is quite enough in any family, I should imagine.'

'Yes, I agree,' Leila said, looking at him bravely. 'I make no excuses for her, but I care about her and she's basically a decent person.'

'Maybe so,' he said. 'Well…goodnight, Leila.'

With that, he turned away abruptly and walked away quickly from her down the corridor, his white lab coat, which he wore over his green scrub suit, flapping around him.

'Oh, hell,' Leila muttered, watching him go, her emotions churning. 'At least that's over. He knows!' Maybe they could both find a way of putting all that behind them. Nonetheless, she felt instinctively that for quite some time she would be on trial, so to speak, where Dr Daniels was concerned.

As she walked hurriedly down the corridor with the trolley of supplies, Leila wondered again why she had blurted all that out about her parents, all that personal stuff about her childhood that she had always tried to keep under wraps with most people. She had tried to present her youthful life as near-perfect—as it should have been, given all that they'd had in the material sense.

Having said all that, she now felt that it somehow created a sort of bond between them, a shared confidence. Don't be stupid, she told herself angrily. How can there be a shared confidence when he hasn't told me anything about himself? But in a way he had, what he had said to her father had revealed a great deal about him. The last thing she wanted was to get involved in any way with a doctor, least of all an obstetrics man, even to the extent of sharing confidences with him. In no time at all you could find yourself emotionally involved. At the same time, she longed for that involvement—with someone. She remembered the feel of the baby in her arms, its soft warmth, the protectiveness that she had felt. Maybe she wanted a baby of her own. Her mind shied away from that.

What her father had said was embarrassing for her. He had treated Dr Daniels like a resident in training or an intern. At the time she had wanted to confront him, to shout at him, 'Go home to your wife. Real life is elsewhere!'

'I was beginning to think you'd decided to go home,' Anne quipped as Leila pushed the trolley of supplies through the door of room six. 'Where have you been for the last fifteen minutes?'

'Just having a few words with…er…Rupert,' she said. 'Sorry.'

'You sneaky thing!' Anne said. 'What happened? You look as red as the proverbial beetroot.'

'I'll tell you in a minute when I've calmed down.'

'And there you were being all cool right here. What do you think of him?'

'It's early days. He seems nice,' she said pensively, evasively. 'One thing in his favour, he doesn't allow himself to be bullied by my father.'

'How come?'

As they distributed the supplies, Leila told her.

'How did your father hear about Dr Daniels's case with the twins?' Anne asked. 'And how come he was here in the operating suite in the evening when he no longer has operating privileges?'

'He must make it his business to find out what's going on in the department,' Leila speculated. 'He thinks he has a right to be anywhere. It wouldn't occur to him to think otherwise.'

Anne voiced what Leila was thinking. 'In which case,' she said, 'he could be an embarrassment if he decided to interfere with decisions made by other doctors.'

'Yes, that's what I'm frightened of,' Leila said.

'Can't you influence him?'

'I can try, although I don't hold out much hope. Rupert Daniels has no reason to scoff,' she went on, 'if that was what he was doing. Five years or so from now he could be in the same mould as my father, juggling work and family—if he has one.'

'I don't think he even has a wife right now, from what I've heard,' Anne said. Then she gave a cackle of cynical laughter. 'Maybe he's too smart.'

'It's nice to have money,' Leila said speculatively, 'but it's not enough.'

In the future, in any relationship with a man, it would not be enough. For herself she wanted something different. One could lose a fortune in one way or another. Then what was left after the years of neglect? She wanted time and companionship, as well as love. She wanted affection and attention. It sounded so simple, but it wasn't.

CHAPTER FOUR

HALF an hour after the ten-to-six nurses had gone home the telephone shrilled in the head nurse's office, and Leila ran to answer it.

'Operating Room. Leila Hardwick, RN, speaking,' she answered breathlessly.

'Hi. This is the emergency triage desk,' a voice announced calmly. 'We have a case coming in by ambulance, a thirty-eight-year-old pregnant woman in labour, thirty-nine weeks pregnant. She's visiting downtown from the suburbs and was involved in a minor car accident. Her husband was driving and neither one of them is actually injured, just shaken up, but she went into labour as a result. Had a previous C-section. It will be Dr Daniels's case, since he's on call.'

'Right,' Leila said. 'I guess it will be another Caesarean.'

'I would guess so. The baby's OK so far, so I understand. The paramedics have put an IV line in. We'll get the obs resident to see her initially down here if there's time, and we'll take some blood for a type and cross-match.'

'Right. We'll be ready.' Leila replaced the receiver, feeling that familiar mixture of excitement and stress, the immediate need to think ahead to all that they would need to be in a state of complete readiness. Room six was ready for such a case.

A thirty-nine-week pregnancy meant that the baby was almost at full term so it had a very good chance of survival, provided that there had been no actual trauma to the uterus and that the placenta—the only source of oxygen for the baby—had not begun to separate prematurely. Now the first priority was to tell Anne.

'Anne!' she bawled down the corridor, ignoring the intercom system that she could have used. 'All systems go! Room six.'

Anne's head popped round a door of one of the operating rooms nearby.

'What?' she said.

'Pregnant woman, thirty-nine weeks, in labour, involved in minor car accident, coming straight up to us! Quick C-section. Baby OK so far. Mother OK.'

'Righty-ho.' The head disappeared.

Leila paged Rupert Daniels, the anaesthetist on call, then Dr Clara Nin, the paediatrician. If the baby was injured after all, they would have to do something about that very quickly. She would have a second surgical set-up on hand too, just in case. The thought of that made her feel slightly sick.

She then called the technologist on call at the blood bank of the hospital to confirm. The nurses in Emergency would send a blood sample to the lab. 'Send the cross-matched blood up to the OR as soon as you have it, please,' Leila said.

Just as she hung up the receiver from that call, one of the other telephones started shrilling. That would be Rupert Daniels returning her page. One after the other the on-call staff called in quickly.

Leila put the main office telephone on call-forward to room six, then hurried down the corridor.

'I've opened the gown pack and put out gloves,' Anne called to her from the scrub sinks as she was about to push open the door to room six. 'And I've opened the other packs. I still need the sponges and the sutures opened up. I've hung up IV Ringer's and a bag of normal saline.'

'OK,' Leila said in passing. Anne was busy soaping her arms and hands at the sinks. She would be the scrub nurse, while she, Leila, would be the circulating nurse in the room. They knew the routine inside out and all ways, she mused as she hurried into the room.

The two powerful arc lamps, suspended from the ceiling, were on over the operating table, the sterile packs and trays of instruments opened, the anaesthetic machine ready with all its associated equipment.

Quickly, yet without undue haste, Leila crossed the room to where the sterile set-up was positioned on the wheeled table and bowl stands, and began methodically to open sterile packs of large gauze sponges, which would be used to soak up blood, and dropped them onto the sterile bowl stand. Then she started on the pile of suture packages, opening each one carefully and dropping the contents—suture material attached to a needle, and ligature material—onto the stand. She would do the basics now, then finish the rest later as things were required.

Anne came into the room, water dripping from her bent arms, and headed for the gown table and the towels there to wipe her hands and arms prior to putting on a sterile gown and latex gloves.

'I thought we wouldn't get through the evening with nothing,' she commented, busily drying her arms. 'We'll get to see what our friend Dr Daniels is like in an emergency. With these accident cases there are often injuries that don't show up immediately, like a slow bleed or something.'

'Mmm,' Leila said, any further comments stifled by the shrilling of the room telephone.

'She's on her way up,' the emergency triage nurse informed her matter-of-factly. 'In the elevator right now.'

'We're ready,' Leila said.

'We took a straight X-ray of the abdomen—the film's coming up with her. The mother's blood pressure's a bit on the low side, and so is the baby's heart rate.'

'OK. Thanks,' Leila said.

'On her way?' Anne asked, methodically setting up her trays and tables of instruments.

'Yep. Sounds as though it's all under control, more or less,' Leila said, as she moved quickly and methodically around the room. Just then the on-call anaesthetist came into the room, tying on a face mask, his black skin glistening with a fine sheen of sweat. 'Hi,' he greeted them with a grin. 'I was part way through the greatest plateful of lasagna I've ever tasted in any hospital cafeteria. Had to leave it behind.'

'It's our lot to go hungry,' Leila smiled back.

Hard on his heels was the obs and gynae intern, a tall, burly young man only in the job two weeks, looking scared. Knowing he was not long out of medical school, Leila moved to put him at his ease.

'Hi, Dr Amos.' She smiled. 'What size gloves do you take?'

'Eights, please,' he said, standing about awkwardly.

'The patient's on her way up,' she said. 'Better get scrubbed right away. You can help the scrub nurse with the prep when the time comes.'

'Right,' he said, relieved to have something definite to do outside the room.

Then came the anaesthetic resident to help the staff man with the mother and baby. Together they began a check of their equipment and began to draw up drugs into syringes.

Anne was well on the way to being ready when Rupert Daniels came in. 'All set, Ms Hardwick?' he asked. He was wearing the ubiquitous two-piece green scrub suit and a cap over his hair.

'Just about,' Leila confirmed, finding herself more than ordinarily self conscious about doing her job efficiently, anxious to anticipate all that would be required.

'Great,' he said with a calm smile, taking in the activity in the room as he tied on a disposable paper face mask and came to stand beside her, his blue eyes assessing her openly. 'I'll get scrubbed. And I'll get to see what the daughter of Geoffrey Hardwick is like when there's a bit of pressure on.'

'So you will, Dr Daniels,' she said. 'And I'll be looking at you, too.'

He smiled, raising his eyebrows at her as he turned to go out of the room. Nonetheless, she felt that there was more behind his words than the obvious meaning, the impression being that he would not be easy on her. Because of her father and her sister, perhaps he felt that he had old scores to settle, and if he was looking for a scapegoat, she would be very conveniently placed. Thoughtfully she looked after him, thinking that surely he would not be that petty.

'Is he flirting with you?' Anne said, her eyes wide, pausing for two seconds in her rush to line up her instruments on the instrument tray that would go over the patient's body.

'Hard to say,' Leila said, 'since I don't know him. Doubt it. Are you ready for the sponge and instrument count?'

'Have we got time?'

'We'll do the sponges, then you'll just have to count the instruments as you go along,' Leila said.

Crashing and banging heralded the opening of the metal elevator doors down the corridor moments later and the stretcher being unloaded and wheeled quickly down the corridor. That was the cue for Leila to go out to do a very quick check on the patient before she was wheeled straight into the room.

'Got all you need for now, Anne?' she asked tersely as she propped open the double doors ready to receive the stretcher.

'Yeah, fine for now.'

Leila hurried out, to see a nurse from Emergency, plus the obs and gynae resident, Dr Chuck Burney, and a porter from Emergency, pushing the stretcher down the main OR corridor. 'In here,' she called to them.

'Help me!' A woman, looking older than her thirty-eight years, lay on the stretcher, her long hair dishevelled, her face pallid. A white towel covering her protuberant abdomen. Two IV lines snaked under the covers.

'The membranes just ruptured in Emergency,' the accompanying nurse said to Leila quietly, 'and the contractions are reasonably strong.'

Leila took the woman's hand as they pushed the stretcher through the doors of room six. 'We're going to help you right now,' she said, trying to put as much reassurance into her voice as she possibly could. 'We're all ready for you.'

'Please...don't let my baby die,' the woman said, a look of entreaty on her pale face, her voice betraying her extreme fear. 'I want this baby. It's my first baby.' She seemed on the edge of hysteria as she gripped Leila's hand hard.

'You're going to be all right,' Dr Chuck Burney reiterated as he held the door open with his shoulder, easing the stretcher through.

'What's her name?' Leila asked him quietly.

'Carmel Agenta,' he said, putting his mouth close to her ear. 'Mrs.'

'Here are the notes and the X-ray films,' the nurse said to Leila, handing over a thin sheaf of records. 'Vital signs are OK on both mother and baby at this moment, but that could change any minute. We didn't have time to get any sort of consent to operate filled out.'

'Help me... Please, help me,' the woman said, looking dazedly around the room into which she was being wheeled, taking in the brilliant lights and strange equipment.

In seconds the stretcher was lined up beside the operating table and many hands helped to move the woman over onto it to position her in the centre and clip a belt around her legs so that she could not fall off.

'Mrs Agenta, you're all right,' Leila repeated, bending down to the woman so that she could be heard above the sudden increased noise level in the room, taking her hand again, squeezing it firmly. 'Just lie quietly and listen to what I and the doctors say to you. That's what you have to do. I'm the nurse. We're going to take the pain away. We're going to give you an anaesthetic and get the baby out as quickly as possible.'

'When did you last eat or drink?' the anaesthetist asked their patient.

'I don't know exactly,' the woman said, casting her eyes around the room. 'Several hours ago. Is my baby going to be all right?'

'All the signs indicate that it will be,' the doctor said. 'Take it easy.'

Dr Daniels was in the room, his surgical gown on, pulling on his latex gloves, with the intern beside him, still looking scared.

'Get scrubbed, Chuck,' Rupert Daniels said to his resident surgeon.

'Right,' Dr Burney said. Both he and the intern would assist with the operation. Just then, Clara Nin came into the room, tying on a face mask, giving a rueful glance to Leila.

Leila moved to tie up the surgeons' gowns while the anaesthetists applied monitors to their patient's chest to record vital signs. 'Take it easy,' the staff anaesthetist said again to the woman on the operating table. 'Everything's under control now. You're OK and the baby's OK.' Then he went on to explain gently what he was doing.

Quickly Leila put the abdominal X-ray plate up on a viewing-box on the wall. It showed the outline of the baby, with no apparent abnormality, as far as she could tell. There could, of course, be soft-tissue damage from the accident, she speculated.

Then she moved to stand beside the operating table to hold their patient's hand while the surgeons stood back, quietly waiting. Mrs Agenta gripped her hand as though she would crush the bones, her wide, staring eyes on Leila's face.

'Breathe some oxygen, Mrs Agenta,' the anaesthetist said calmly, bringing a clear plastic mask down close to the woman's face. 'This is for both you and the baby. It won't put you to sleep, so just take deep, even breaths.'

'My baby, my baby…' the woman moaned, tears dribbling down her face. 'Don't let anything happen to it—please. Do I have to have that thing on my face?'

With her free hand Leila held the mask a fraction of an inch above the woman's face. 'No,' she said, 'I'll just hold it.'

She well understood the feeling of claustrophobia a patient could feel from having a mask firmly clamped over their nose and mouth, especially when they were feeling panic-stricken about their condition and chances of survival, frightened by the unfamiliar atmosphere of the operating suite, with its brilliant lights, unidentifiable gowned and masked figures, tables of instruments and equipment.

In moments their patient would be under the anaesthetic. Normally they would do the skin prep for a C-section while the woman was still awake, to lessen the time that the baby could be affected by the anaesthetic agents, but because this woman had been traumatized by the accident, they wanted to have her unconscious as quickly as possible. Then they would move fast.

Rupert Daniels and Anne were ready to do the skin prep. Leila found that, again, she was uncommonly aware of him waiting quietly and patiently very close to her, sensitive to him because he had touched her. It was a reluctant feeling, and it was as though she could still feel the mark of his warm fingers under her chin and on her bare arm. No time to wonder why.

He stood perfectly still, holding a small stainless-steel pot in one hand, which held Betadine, the iodine prep solution, and a long metal sponge holder, with a gauze sponge gripped in it, in the other hand. To Leila he seemed totally calm, almost detached. That was the mark of a good surgeon. Many of the mediocre ones ranted and raved at members of the staff, perhaps in the hope of drawing attention away from themselves and what they were not able to do. Irritated with herself for being so sensitive to his presence, she concentrated extra hard on what was going on right in front of her.

It was important to get that baby out as quickly as possible.

The anaesthesia resident connected the foetal monitor.

A sound like a bellows operating under water, the heart-beat of the unborn child, filled the room. 'Your baby's all right, Mrs Agenta,' he said.

'Are you sure?' came the muffled, frightened reply. All the time Leila squeezed her hand.

'Quite sure,' he said.

Leila knew that the heart rate was just within normal range, but slower than they would have liked.

Slickly the anaesthetist injected the anaesthetic drugs into an IV line and in seconds the woman had closed her eyes, while the anaesthesia resident moved to assist with the intubation, putting a tube into the woman's trachea, through which the anaesthetic gases and the oxygen would pass for the duration of the operation.

In moments the patient was cleaned and draped with sterile green sheets by Rupert, with the help of Chuck Burney and the intern, Greg Amos. Quickly Leila pushed Anne's sterile set-up into place beside the operating table, then efficiently connected the ends of the diathermy lead and the suction tubing that Anne passed to her. There would be a lot of blood and amniotic fluid from the uterus as the baby was being delivered, which had to be suctioned out.

'All right to cut?' Rupert asked the anaesthetist.

'Go ahead.'

'Knife, please,' Rupert said to Anne.

The operation was under way.

CHAPTER FIVE

'KEEP up the suction, please, Greg,' Rupert said as the top of the baby's head appeared, dark and coated with clotted blood, in the aperture created by the incision in the lower segment of the uterus. 'Give me a little bit of fundal pressure, Chuck...gently.'

Greg was sweating, his face pink, working to control a gush of amniotic fluid that had escaped from the uterus moments before. He deployed the suction to clear away the fluid and blood, while Anne passed up large gauze sponges for the same purpose. Chuck applied some pressure to the top of the uterus, where the baby's bottom was lying, to help ease the head through the incision.

While Leila stood near the operating table, watching progress, the baby's head emerged slowly through the opening, eased out carefully by the gloved hands of Rupert. One shoulder was out, then the other. 'Ready with the cord clamps,' he said.

Gently, with practised ease, he lifted the body of the baby out of the cut uterus, gripping it firmly by the ankles as the legs appeared, and laid it down, with its head lower than its body to drain mucus from the nose and mouth so that it could breathe without inhaling fluid.

'It's a boy,' he said. 'So far, so good. He's got all his fingers and toes, by the look of it. Come on, little guy, give us a sound or two.' With a small surgical towel he vigorously wiped the baby's body to stimulate him.

They all took a hurried look at the baby before attending to tasks in hand, sharing in the collective relief. The baby slowly lifted up his tiny arms and opened his mouth in preparation for the first cry, the first breath.

With a clean gauze sponge Rupert quickly wiped the baby's nose and mouth to clear them of mucus and fluid, while Clara Nin approached with a suction tube and apparatus for the purpose of clearing the baby's airway.

'Clamps, Dr Burney,' Anne said, passing Chuck two large metal clamps to clamp off the umbilical cord attaching the baby to the placenta. The cord was thick, slippery and gelatinous, a darkish blue-grey in colour with a glistening grey-white transparent outer layer. 'Scissors.'

Chuck clamped the cord in two places, several centimetres apart, then cut between the two, thus separating the baby from the placenta and making the final separation between baby and mother. It all took a few seconds only. The baby, large and healthy-looking, began to make small crying noises. It was an encouraging sound, and Leila smiled, exchanging relieved glances with Anne. One hurdle was over.

'Atta boy!' Chuck said, lifting up the baby by head and feet. 'He looks good. Ready to take him, Dr Nin?'

'I sure am.'

As Clara took him to place him in the sterile resuscitation cart, the baby flung up his tiny arms, took a gurgling breath and let out several loud cries, again bringing smiles all round. With the sound filling the room, the surgical team turned their attention back to the mother. The first priority now was to deliver the placenta and stop any unnecessary loss of blood from the uterus. The anaesthetist began to inject the drugs that would make the uterus contract, while Rupert put his hand inside the uterus to gently remove the placenta.

Leila made up two name tags for the baby, one to be affixed to his wrist and one around his ankle. She also wrote on the operation sheet, 'Live male birth.' Letting out a pent-up breath, she allowed herself to relax a little.

'There doesn't seem to be any damage to the uterus from the car accident, as far as I can see so far,' Rupert said. 'We'll get a better look when the placenta's out.'

'What I could use now,' Anne whispered to Leila as she came close, 'is a good, strong, sweet cup of black coffee.'

'Ditto,' Leila said, *sotto voce.*

All the time the baby kept up a lusty cry while Clara efficiently went about her business of taking care of him. I wish I could gather him up in my arms, Leila thought. No time for that. Right now they had to concentrate on looking after his mother. At least *his* mother would love him, would welcome him with relief and joy. What a strange world it was, the wanted and the unwanted, the adored and the ignored, and all the shades in between those two extremes. In Gresham General they saw it all.

On with the next thing. It didn't do to brood too much. It was going to be a busy evening, right up to the time that the night nurses came on duty. They were people of action in the OR. You used your skills, your training, your experience. You did what you could.

Room six looked as though a minor hurricane had hit it by the time the operation was finished and the patient had been wheeled out to the recovery room.

'We got through it, Anne!' Leila said to her colleague tiredly as the patient disappeared from view, accompanied by the two anaesthetists and the junior surgeons. 'I'm absolutely pooped.'

'You can say that again,' Anne said. 'My feet ache, my legs ache, my whole body aches. As soon as I get these dirty instruments sorted out I'm going to have that coffee

I've been promising myself and craving for, even if it means that I don't sleep for the rest of the night. After that, I can't wait to get out into the fresh air—relatively fresh, that is.'

'What a mess,' Leila said, standing with her hands on her hips, surveying the scene. 'It could have been worse for her. She could have had a ruptured uterus, being in a car accident.'

'Yes, she's very lucky,' Anne commented as she sorted through dirty instruments. 'And what a gorgeous baby.'

'Mmm. I wish he were mine.'

'There's no need to lust after other people's babies,' a voice said from the doorway. 'You are most likely capable of having your own. That's the advantage that women have over men.'

'Oh, Dr Daniels,' Leila said, turning to face the owner of the voice, feeling an unwelcome frisson of awareness that was becoming familiar, 'you're listening to our conversation again.' This was dangerous territory.

'It's an occupational hazard in this department,' he said, coming into the room. 'There's no privacy here. I just wanted to thank you for your expert help.'

'Anything else pending?' Anne asked.

'Not that I know of,' he said.

'We're going to be making coffee soon, Dr Daniels,' Anne said pertly, 'in about twenty minutes, so if you and the other guys want some, just come into the coffee-room then.'

'Thank you, I could use some coffee,' he said.

It was good to leave the main work area a little later on to go to the coffee-lounge in the department, outside the main work area. As she left, Leila tore off the disposable paper face mask she had kept dangling around her neck, together with the soft paper hat that covered her hair, and threw them into a bin for the purpose. Thankfully she ran a hand through her short blonde hair, enjoying the feel of air on her scalp again. In the coffee-room she eased her feet out of her slip-on shoes, welcoming the effect of the cold tiles on her aching feet. The floor had recently been washed by the cleaning staff.

'Ah!' She let out a sigh of pleasure, then took a deep breath and let it out slowly again, willing the stress to leave her and her tense shoulder muscles to relax.

Meeting Rupert Daniels had been an ordeal really, as soon as she had known that he was the one her sister had pursued relentlessly. The mortification was difficult to bear. How could a woman—particularly one as beautiful and talented as Stacey, who had never had any difficulty in getting boyfriends—continue to pursue a man who had clearly not been interested in her. Although at the time Leila had not known all the details, that much she had understood.

With a practised hand she made coffee in the urn that they kept there for that purpose. That would be for the staff who did not have the luxury of being able to go to bed for the night. As the pleasant aroma filled the room she got out mugs and a packet of cookies, which she emptied out on to a plate, all the while flexing her toes deliciously on the cold floor. Then she made tea for herself, knowing that coffee would keep her awake.

One by one the junior doctors drifted in to drink a quick cup of coffee and eat a few cookies. They were the ones on call for the remainder of the night, would most likely be working, while she and Anne could go home to sleep. For that reason she didn't mind the evening shift.

'How's the patient doing?' Leila asked Chuck as he gulped his coffee. He was tall, raw-boned, ginger-haired.

'She seems OK so far. Her vitals are stable,' he said. 'And the baby's fine, too, much to his mother's relief.'

As he had been speaking, Rupert had come into the room, closely followed by Anne. Leila could tell by the smile on Anne's face that she had been talking to him. As he came in he looked at Leila intently, his eyes going over her hair and face, then down to her stockinged feet. This was the first time that he had seen her without her head and face coverings, and Leila realized with a sense of shock that he was most likely comparing her with her beautiful sister. There was definitely a resemblance in colouring between them, and something about the eyes, but apart from that they were not a lot alike. His scrutiny renewed the sense of vulnerability she had been feeling from the moment she had realized his identity, especially as she detected what she interpreted as a certain cynicism in his regard. Trying not to show it, she concentrated on sipping her tea.

It had been clear from what Stacey had told her in the past that Rupert had been very attracted to her but had not allowed himself to get involved with her—those were Stacey's words. Now, as he looked at her, and she felt herself become slightly uncomfortable under his scrutiny, she could somehow believe that Stacey had been telling the truth. What responsible man after all, she told herself, would sire a child and them walk away? Perhaps Stacey had been angling for marriage and had used her desire to have a baby as a reason to hide the fact.

Either way, Leila now felt a tide of embarrassment beginning to flood over her, as though she were in some way responsible for the past actions of her supposedly more mature sister. As well as Stacey, there was the question of her father, hanging around the hospital, looking to make trouble, when he should be retiring gracefully, making a life for himself outside of the hospital. If anyone had a reason to start off on the wrong foot with this new doctor, it was her. All the more reason, she told herself, to go very, very carefully.

'Is…is the baby all right, Dr Daniels?' she asked. The baby had been taken up to the neonatal intensive care unit, she knew that. 'Chuck just said he was all right, but he *was* a little slow to cry after delivery.'

'He seems fine so far,' Rupert said, turning away from her to help himself to coffee. 'Dr Nin is taking good care of him. We'll ship him off to Children's Hospital if there's a hint that he needs to be there.'

'Good,' Leila said. 'Help yourself to coffee, Dr Amos.'

Greg Amos, the intern, whom Leila was beginning to think of as the gentle giant, looked exhausted as he sat in a battered armchair with his feet on an equally battered coffee-table that was strewn with dog-eared newspapers.

Leila smiled at him. 'Did you enjoy that case?' she asked.

He coloured slightly. 'I'm not sure that "enjoy" is the right word,' he said slowly, thoughtfully, as he got to his feet. 'And since this is my first training rotation, I'm not sure that surgery is my forte. Maybe I'm better at delivering babies in the usual way.'

'You were really great, Greg. I've been meaning to tell you,' Rupert said. 'You stick close to Chuck here and he'll teach you a lot about surgery as it relates to obstetrics.'

'Thanks.'

It was pleasant in the cosy coffee-room, an oasis from the realities of the actual operating rooms, and Leila found herself relaxing in spite of Rupert Daniels being very close by. Not for one moment could she forget the presence of the new doctor.

*   *   *

When eleven-fifteen came, with the arrival of the night nurses, Leila was ready for them. It was a relief to get out.

In the nurses' locker room Leila changed into her street clothes, then walked to the elevator in the corridor outside the operating rooms that would take her to the ground floor and the way out to the car park where she had left her car.

As the elevator came and she was about to get into it, her father came out. Surprised to see him in the middle of the night, she was momentarily speechless.

'Oh, hello, dear,' he said to her. 'Just going home?' He stood before her, his hands thrust into the pockets of a slightly grubby lab coat that he wore over street clothes— the formal dark blue suit and striped shirt, with tie, that he usually wore around the hospital. His grey hair was longish, a little untidy, and he looked tired.

'Dad!' she said. 'What are you doing here at…' she consulted her watch '…ten minutes to midnight?' As she asked the question she had the proverbial sinking feeling that he had been there stirring up trouble for Rupert. At the same time she felt a sadness and something akin to pity that he was not at home, trying to enjoy a life outside this place. As for herself, now that her shift was over, she couldn't wait to get out.

'Oh, just doing a few necessary things,' he said, looking at her sideways, a little slyly. 'There's still an awful lot to do around here one way and another. I have two patients in here right now, have to see those.'

Leila knew that he did not have admitting privileges now that he had retired, and the patients he considered his had most likely been admitted by another doctor, even though they might want to continue to see him outside.

Tactfully, she refrained from letting him know she realized that. After all, he was not incompetent—a doctor did not suddenly become no good when he reached a certain age. There were good and bad doctors of all ages. Yet as she stood looking at him, feeling a familiar ache of love for him in spite of his emotional distance, she wished he would just go gracefully from the hospital setting.

Voices came to them from around a corner, at which her father became a little agitated, conspiratorial. 'Must go, dear,' her father said. 'Don't want to bump into that upstart Daniels. See you on the weekend, dear…maybe.'

'Yes,' she said. 'Dad, please don't alienate Dr Daniels. It's really nothing to do with you what he does with his patients. Please. He's a good surgeon, a good doctor. I've just been working with him, so I know. And, Dad…Mum needs you. Think about that…please.'

Without replying, her father walked away.

From the other direction two nurses came by and walked on down the corridor, and behind them was Rupert. At the sight of him, Leila felt her face colour slightly, as though she had been caught out somehow as she saw him look after her retreating father.

'Ms. Hardwick,' he said, inclining his head towards her. Like all of them, he looked tired.

Leila nodded.

In silence they waited for the elevator. There was no one else about now, no sound. Then he said, 'How *is* Stacey?'

'She's well,' Leila said, willing the elevator to come. 'We just spent a holiday together. Usually I don't see her much. She's in the States now, in Houston.'

'Is she liking it?' he said. She wished he wouldn't look at her so intently.

'Yes, very much.' Then unthinkingly she added, 'I

don't suppose she'll come back to Gresham.' When she met his eyes, there was a somewhat amused, cynical expression in them as he raised his eyebrows.

'Just as well perhaps,' he said, giving her a slow, wry smile. 'For the male population of the city. Is she a mother yet? Married?'

With burning cheeks, Leila stared back at him. 'No to both of those questions,' she said, fighting to keep her voice even. 'I hope you won't let those past happenings distort our professional relationship, Dr Daniels. Stacey was naïve and immature at the time.'

'She was thirty,' he said. Leila got the impression that he had been waiting to corner her like this, on her own in an empty corridor.

'Yes, well, she'd led a privileged life. She thought that what she wanted would just fall into her lap...I guess,' Leila said. 'I really don't know what motivated her. Anyway, I apologize for her, in case she didn't do it for herself at the time. As I said earlier, I'm not like my sister.'

'Yet you have strong views, Ms Hardwick,' he said. 'I couldn't help overhearing your discussion with your colleague on marriage.'

'Those views have nothing to do with you, Dr Daniels, and, as Anne said, they're very much theoretical ideas which I'm not about to try to put into practice in the way that my sister did.'

'Glad to know that,' he said, pressing his lips together as though he was trying not to smile. For some reason that infuriated her, striking her as supercilious.

'You have strong views, too, Dr Daniels,' she countered. 'And you obviously take action on those views.'

'Professionally, yes. Do you object?'

'No, they are nothing to do with me, although I think

I would have done the same in your position…if I'd had the courage to act on my beliefs, that is,' she said, trying to be fair. 'And I dissociate myself from anything my father might say or do.'

'As you dissociate yourself from your sister?' he said.

'Yes. This may sound rude—it's not meant to be,' she said, rushing on. 'You can rest assured that I'm not after you in any way, so I hope you won't feel that I'm a predatory woman waiting to pounce. Unlike my sister, the last person I want is a medical man. You see, Stacey really did have the attitude that anything she wanted she was entitled to get, even a particular man. For once she wanted something that Daddy's money could not buy.'

There was a moment of rather awful silence while Rupert appeared to digest what she had said, and she stood in shock at what she had had the temerity to utter. The annoyance that she felt was more associated with her sister.

'That's good,' he said, 'because I'm not on offer.'

'Good.' Her lips felt stiff.

'Could your sister be why your father has such anti-pathy towards me?' he asked tightly.

'I don't think so. He didn't really know much about it. She didn't confide in him,' Leila said.

Before she could say anything else, the elevator arrived, the doors opening noisily to reveal a person in there, a cleaner with a bulky cart of cleaning materials, mops and brooms. Leila took up a position at the back of the elevator, looking at the floor.

They all got out on the ground floor, a short walk from the main entrance lobby where she would exit to go to her car.

'Wait, please,' he said to her, while the cleaner slowly trundled her cart away out of earshot. There were only a few people about in the wide corridors that they could view from the empty lobby. Leila stood awkwardly, waiting.

'The best thing for both of us, I think,' he said quietly, 'would be for us to forget about your sister and your father. Agreed? Until I realized who you were, I had put her out of my mind.'

Leila took a deep breath. 'Agreed,' she said. 'I'm sorry if I seemed rude, although I stand by what I said.'

'So be it. I think we know where we stand now. Goodnight, Ms Hardwick,' he said, with no particular inflection in his voice.

'Goodnight,' she muttered, not looking at him, turning swiftly for the exit. So that was that.

Well, she had told him, she said to herself as she marched away. That, hopefully, had cleared the air. From now on they should be able to build a professional relationship. It was a relief to have the inevitable confrontation finished with.

What she hadn't told Rupert was that maybe she and her siblings—including her two brothers—had received almost everything of a material nature that they wanted, like many other children in professional families, but what they had craved had been love and attention from a father. Perhaps it would not have been so bad if there had been no father. Having one, they had expected something of him, more than he had been prepared to give. He had wanted children, had taken delight in them as babies, so her mother had said, then had found he had been unable to cope as they had got older and more complex. He had tried in his way, she supposed. It had not been enough.

Unexpectedly, tears pricked her eyes as she approached the large rotating glass doors to get to the outside. Perhaps Stacey had thought that to have a child without a father would save that child from the burden and frustration of unmet expectations. What Stacey had craved for herself as a woman, Leila thought she could understand now, had been love and attention from a man whom she had felt she could love also, if temporarily. Perhaps she had gone about it in too much of a direct and unorthodox way with Rupert Daniels, and he had spurned her.

Stacey had been such a cute little kid and older girl, with her pale beauty of fair hair and blue eyes, with a little of the tomboy about her and a smattering of freckles across her nose and cheeks. As the oldest of four, she had perhaps been very aware that parental attention had to go a long way. As she had got older she had become more calculating, going after what she had wanted with single-minded dedication.

Leila acknowledged that she herself was more realistic in going after what she wanted where men were concerned. She knew herself to be calm on the outside but soft in the centre, a vulnerability that she tried not to show too much. Certainly it was something that she would not show to the watchful Rupert Daniels, who was 'not on offer'. There was an arrogance in that, she fumed now as she thought about their verbal exchange. At the same time, she had to admire him for his forthrightness.

Yet there had been something rather jarring in his attitude, something that seemed to come from more than her sister's failed relationship with him. That sense created an unease in her.

Well, she wanted to put all that out of her mind now that her sister was far away. And if Rupert Daniels thought he was God's gift to women, that he was totally desirable, then she for one would disabuse him.

CHAPTER SIX

LEILA found that it was raining heavily when she pushed through the huge doors to the covered portico of the main entrance to the hospital to go to the parking lot, where her car was out in the open nearby, where she liked to park in the evening. It was well lit, almost as clear as day. Turning up the collar of her short raincoat, she plunged into it, enjoying the feel of the rain on her face after being in the confines of the operating room.

The car engine made an ineffectual whirring sound when she turned the ignition key, repeating itself several times. 'Oh, damn,' she muttered. Maybe water had got into the engine. Judging from the size of the puddles around, there had been an awful lot of rain.

For several minutes she sat there trying the engine, pumping the accelerator with her foot.

It was no good. She would just have to go back into the hospital and call for a taxi, or see if she had the jump-leads in the boot, which she had not used for a long time. Maybe if someone else came out of the hospital to a car near her own, she could get a boost from them. Not much of a hope, as there was no one else about.

'Damn!' she said again, as she looked into the boot, trying to shelter as best she could under the cover. The boot contained nothing but a few old newspapers. She must have put the leads somewhere else when she had last cleaned the car.

'Trouble?' a voice said as she withdrew from under cover into the drenching rain.

For a few seconds she didn't recognize Rupert as he stood near her car, his dark hair wet, a long raincoat enveloping him almost down to his ankles, the collar turned up. The garment gave him a slightly rakish air.

So unexpected was his appearance that Leila could not immediately think of anything to say. She had assumed that he would be sleeping at the hospital. But, no, he was a staff man and could go home if he was not needed immediately. His senior resident, Chuck, would deal with anything in the first instance.

'I...um,' she said, while the wind and rain lashed at her face.

'Won't start?' he ventured.

'Um...no. Must be wet.'

'Let me give you a ride home,' he said. 'I'm parked just here.'

'Oh, you don't have to,' she said.

'I know I don't have to,' he countered, as they stood close together, getting wetter by the second.

'Do you have any jump-leads?'

'No.'

Because she was so tired, it seemed to be happening in a dream that he opened the door of a car that was parked two spaces down from her own, that she got in quickly out of the rain, that he was beside her. 'I could get a taxi,' she said.

'So you could.'

'Shall I?'

'No.'

Leila turned to him. 'I know you don't like my father or my sister. So, by extension, I expect you're pretty apathetic about me. The last thing I want to do is impose myself on you, so why are you giving me a ride?'

'Something to do with the damsel in distress,' he said,

looking at her sideways with an unreadable expression. 'It's an automatic reaction.'

'I'm not in distress,' she said. 'I'm pretty good at looking after myself.' That wasn't strictly true, as she was desperate to get home.

He paused in starting the car. 'Let's just say that I'm intrigued by a woman who states that she's not interested in me.'

'That must be a new experience for you, Dr Daniels,' she said flatly.

'Not entirely new,' he said slowly. 'It just hasn't been couched in quite those terms.'

'I assumed you would be very happy with that,' she said. 'And I assume that the sentiment is mutual.'

Rupert shrugged in what seemed to her to be a rather eloquent gesture, his attractive face carefully controlled, not denying her assumption. In spite of her antipathy to him, she had to admit that he had a certain style that could be engaging...to some women.

Just then a flash of lightning lit up the interior of the car brilliantly, followed almost immediately by a loud clap of thunder. Leila swallowed a nervous lump in her throat. 'Oh, I hate lightning,' she said. 'It scares me. I...do appreciate the ride.'

'This must be making up for the drought we've had,' he said, turning to her so that she could see raindrops glistening on his face. 'It looks as though there's going to be a terrific storm. What will you do about your car?'

'Oh...I suppose I'll bring some jump-leads tomorrow, see if it'll start. Or I'll call the automobile association. They'll get it towed. It's a pretty old car. Secondhand,' she said, feeling that this must be one of the most stilted conversations she'd ever had. Leila shut her mouth, clutched her wet handbag to her chest, waiting for the next flash of lightning, and stared out through his car window, having noted the luxurious interior of what was a very expensive European model.

'Where do you live?' he asked.

'Oh—go west on Old College Street.' She waved an ineffectual hand. 'I'll direct you as we go along.' She moved close to the door so that she was as far away from him as possible.

'Right,' he said. The engine of his car started on the first try, of course, a muted purring sound like a contented giant cat. In moments they were out of the parking lot, up a side street and onto Old College Street. Rain lashed the windows in a renewed downpour, reducing visibility to almost nil.

'This is like the monsoon,' she said, feeling compelled to utter something so as not to seem boorish.

'Have you experienced the monsoon?' he said gently.

'No,' she said, with a somewhat hysterical desire to laugh. He had a way of reducing her to nothing, she noted. 'Have you?'

'No. Not yet.'

'Does that mean you'll be going away soon?' she ventured innocently.

'Not in the foreseeable future,' he said. 'How long have you worked at Gresham General?'

'Long enough,' she said shortly. And now that you're there, she wanted to add, it may very soon be too long. She had a prescient feeling that he could read her thoughts.

'You like it there?' he persisted, sounding as though he was smiling, albeit reluctantly. She didn't look at him to see.

'I did until very recently,' she said.

At that he laughed, then fell silent as he concentrated on driving.

While lightning flashed around them, the car crawled along Old College Street, together with a few other late night drivers.

'Go as far as Convent Street,' she said. 'Make a right there. I hope this isn't taking you out of your way.'

'Not much,' he said.

When visibility was almost down to zero, Rupert pulled into a parking lot. 'This is an all-night pub and restaurant, quite good,' he said. 'We may as well stay here for a while. There's no point in risking an accident. Would you like a drink? They make a good hot toddy here.'

Leila nodded, glad that she wasn't driving. 'Well, it's not really cold enough for a hot toddy, but it sounds good.'

'I'm glad you think so.'

They ran the few yards to the entrance of what was a sophisticated restaurant and bar. As Leila caught sight of herself in a mirror in the entrance hall she speculated that she must look at that moment the least sophisticated of the women he had most likely brought there.

'Good evening, Dr Daniels. What a night, eh?' the head waiter greeted her companion. 'Madame,' he added, with a nod in her direction. 'May I take your coats?'

'Thanks,' she said, divesting herself of her dripping raincoat to reveal tight blue jeans, wet around the ankles, and a simple, light sweater. Her shoes squelched as she moved.

Rupert looked her over quickly, a very masculine appraisal that made her intensely aware of how she must look to him. In an understated way, he managed to look smart and sexy himself now that he had taken off his long raincoat, dressed in a casual black turtleneck shirt, dark grey trousers, and a lightweight tweed jacket. Glancing at him surreptitiously, she took in the details of his appearance. Leila had the disconcerting feeling that he was amused by her.

'I don't feel much like a "madame",' Leila said brightly as the waiter moved away ahead of them, determined to be as normal as possible with Rupert in this enforced encounter, assuming that he wanted to get home as much as she did.

'You'll do,' he said.

That was the nearest he had come to paying her a personal compliment, though he had praised her at work in a very professional way. Those simple words made her feel soft and vulnerable.

The bar was dim and cosy, with an unseasonal log fire roaring in an open grate. 'What can I get you?' the waiter asked. 'May I suggest a hot toddy, with brandy?'

'Yes...please,' Leila said, wiping strands of wet hair from her forehead, from which drops of water were dripping down into her eyes.

'I'll have one with just a dash of brandy, since I'm driving,' Rupert said.

'All right, sir. Please, be seated.' They were shown to two armchairs by the fire off the bar area, which was separate from the restaurant where people still sat at tables.

As Leila subsided into the comfortable chair, felt the warmth of the fire, she conceded that this was a very nice place. She had gone by it many times but had never been in. Her friends tended to favour the more trendy places, where they could see and be seen. There was something discreet about this place.

'This place is an interesting mix of the formal and the informal,' she commented. 'I admire your taste.'

'Grudgingly, though,' he said, smiling slightly.

'No, not at all.' That thought made her wonder again about her sister. Evidently, Stacey had not been to his taste. Again she had the feeling that he had intuitively tuned in to her thoughts, and her cheeks felt hot suddenly.

Now that they were sitting near each other, she couldn't think of anything else to say. He became silent also, seeming under no strain to break that silence. Outside, the lightning continued to flash, while the lighting in the bar was dim, the flames of the fire throwing flickering shadows on the walls and furniture, giving the whole scene a surreal air. In spite of being so tensely aware of the man near her, Leila felt herself relax as she stared into the flames. They might have been the only occupants of a large sitting room in an old manor house.

Nonetheless, it was a relief when the drinks came. Hers came with a small pot of honey so that she could sweeten it, which she did.

'This is very nice,' she ventured, again not wishing to appear boorish, as she deplored that trait in others. When she glanced at him, he was looking at her in what seemed to her a very discerning way.

'Yes, it is,' he said. 'And it's good to get out of the hospital for a bit, to have something approaching a normal life for a while. Long enough to recharge one's mental batteries anyway.'

Leila nodded. 'Mmm,' she said thoughtfully. 'I wish my father had more of that turn of mind. It's not easy to balance our kind of work with what we think of as a normal life. You have to constantly make an effort, I think.'

'And what do you do, Leila, to find a balance?' he asked, leaning back in his comfortable chair, looking more attractive than was good for any man, she thought defensively.

'I try to mix with non-medical people—not easy,' she said. 'My dad has a boat and I go out on that on Lake Ontario, I play tennis and squash, go for long walks. My mother has a cabin on an island...I go there. I like the theatre, films, reading. This city has a lot to offer. So I take full advantage of that. I like the restaurants, cafés, wine bars...'

'You sound like a well-rounded person,' he murmured.

'I try to be. What about you?' she asked, glancing at a nearby window to see the state of the weather. Rain still lashed against the glass furiously.

'Don't worry, Leila,' he said. 'The storm will come to an end. You won't have to endure me for too long.'

'I don't mind enduring you,' she said quickly, knowing that her voice sounded false. 'Really.'

'Liar,' he said, smiling.

That smile made her heart do a little flip again. With something approaching a feeling of panic, she realized that she was much more susceptible to Rupert's charm than she had thought herself to be. In her memory she heard Stacey's voice 'I've met this gorgeous man...'

That was no good, being susceptible to someone who was 'not on offer', as he had put it so bluntly. 'You haven't answered my question,' she said.

'I like all those things that you've mentioned,' he said. 'I don't own a boat, but do have friends with boats. It's good to get away, out on the lake and down the St Lawrence River.'

'Why did you choose obstetrics?' she asked, emboldened by the warm glow of brandy, which was doing something positive for her inhibitions, she noted.

'I finally decided when I was in my last year in med

school,' he said. 'I did quite a bit of volunteer work in downtown clinics that took care of very poor and home-less people…I saw the women and the babies, the little kids, who somehow fell through the cracks in the social services of this very wealthy city. I decided then and there to do something about it. I've also volunteered in South America.'

'You still work in the downtown clinics?'

'Yes. As a volunteer…when I can. Generally, they call me when they need a consultation.'

Leila nodded. 'I see,' she said, trying to imagine him as a young medical student, serious and dedicated. 'It's great that you've been able to follow through. A lot of people talk but don't take action.'

How different Rupert was from her father, who had drawn the majority of his patients from the most wealthy of the city, apart from those few women who had arrived at the emergency department when he had been on call, whom he had been obliged to treat. Many of those women had not bothered to seek any antenatal care, or had not known how to get it. They just turned up at a hospital when labour started. From those few he had, no doubt, developed his ideas about 'keeping the family together', where there was no family or proper home.

Rupert took a mouthful of his drink and leaned forward, putting his elbows on his knees. 'It also compensates,' he said slowly, 'for the strong probability that I shall not have a child of my own.'

'Oh… Why?' she blurted out.

For a moment or two he was silent, weighing up his answer. 'Let me just say that it doesn't seem to be hap-pening.'

'But you're not old,' she said. 'You can't be more than…more than…'

'Thirty-five?' he said.

'Something like that.' She seemed to be standing back, watching herself ask those personal questions that she would not have dreamed of asking him in the coffee-room in the OR. Here in this bar, with the warmth of the brandy inside her, she somehow felt like a different person, even as she warned herself not to get into dangerous territory. Perhaps he couldn't have children, perhaps that was why he had been so standoffish with Stacey...

'That's what I am—thirty-five,' he said.

'Well...'

'I have yet to meet a woman whose motives are in sync with mine,' he said.

It was not her imagination that there was a bitterness in his tone, Leila thought as she stared at him. Not knowing what to say, she distracted herself by pushing strands of damp hair away from her forehead.

'I've noticed,' she said at length, as though an invisible prompt were putting the words into her mouth, 'that you don't do so-called therapeutic abortions. Most of the other gynaecologists and obstetricians do.'

'That's right,' he said.

'May I ask why?' she said. 'If you don't think I'm intruding.'

'It's something I'd rather not do myself,' he said, 'although I respect a woman's right to have one. I simply refer those patients to someone else.'

Although he spoke without any particular inflection in his voice, Leila again sensed strong undercurrents of emotion in him.

'I understand,' she said, respecting his honesty in telling her. Some men ranted and raved about the issue, while he simply stated an inability to perform in such a way. 'I can identify with that.'

The obvious unspoken question hung between them, bringing a tension that increased until she could not prevent herself from speaking. These were issues that confronted them every day at work. 'I don't think I could ever bring myself to have one,' she said quietly, 'but I don't condemn those who do.'

'It's a debate that tends to go round in circles,' he said.

They finished their drinks in silence.

'You'll be glad to know,' he said, after he had paid the waiter for the drinks, 'that the rain has stopped and you don't have to endure my company any longer, Leila. May I call you Leila?'

'Yes,' she said, thinking, against her will, how sweetly old-fashioned he was to ask if he could use her first name. A lot of people took the liberty anyway, whether they felt particularly friendly towards you or not.

'Call me Rupert,' he said.

'I can't think of you as a Rupert,' she confessed.

'What could you think of me as?' he asked, grinning slightly.

That grin disarmed her. 'Maybe one of those names that are usually given to the bad guy in a whodunnit novel— Oscar, or Max.'

'Hell,' he said. 'Am I a bad guy?'

'You could be,' she said.

'Because of what you think I did to Stacey? The rejection bit?' he said.

Leila looked at him quickly, then away again. Once more they were getting into deep water. 'Maybe,' she said, shrugging. 'I'm not really sure why.'

'Don't prejudge, Leila,' he said quietly. 'There's a lot that you don't know and can't know.'

'About you?'

'Yes. And a lot of other things besides,' he said gently. 'Tell me, what's wrong with Rupert?'

The brandy was getting to her, loosening her tongue. 'It's too...er...cuddly...or something,' she said consideringly.

He bit his lip and squinted at her thoughtfully, saying nothing.

'You know—Rupert bear,' she added.

'And you don't think of me as cuddly?' he stated. 'I see.'

'No.'

'Well put, Ms Hardwick,' he said with a smile. 'That is very reassuring.'

Again, that smile unnerved her. 'Great,' she said.

'Shall we go?' he said, standing up.

'I hate to think what time it is,' she said, talking more to herself than to him. 'I'm not going to look. I think I'll sleep for the whole weekend.'

'You must be exhausted,' he said.

'Thank you very much for the drink,' she said.

At the doorway Leila declined to put on her wet raincoat again, as did he. The night was fresh, blustery now, the rain gone, leaving huge puddles here and there and water rushing down the gutters at the sides of the street. 'I like this sort of night,' she said, walking beside him to his car, taking in deep breaths. 'When it's relatively fresh for the centre of a city. Nice time to go for a long walk.' Aware that the brandy had made her mellow, she walked and spoke carefully. Now she couldn't wait to get home, to put her feet up and her head down.

Once at her house, she got out of the car quickly, finding his proximity unnerving. Her house was only about a mile and a half away from the hospital.

'Goodnight…er, Rupert,' she said. 'I appreciate the ride.'

'Goodnight,' he said.

Leila felt the tension drain away from her as she let herself into her small garden. It had been a very long, eventful evening.

CHAPTER SEVEN

'HOME,' Leila breathed the word to herself as she often did on arriving. The stresses of work dropped from her when she contemplated the cosy brick façade of her home, with its magenta front door which she had painted herself, complemented by the lion's head brass knocker. Thanks to some help from her parents with the down-payment, a loan, she had managed to raise a mortgage on the rest.

The cottage had two bedrooms on a second floor, and a sitting room and kitchen on the main floor. Lights that had come on with timers, plus the sound of a radio, greeted her as she went inside. She planned to make herself a cup of tea, then have a bath and go to bed. There were two messages on her voice-mail, one from her friend Rory, making tentative plans for the weekend.

As she later sat in the bath and sipped tea she thought about her own life, about her lack of a serious man friend. Sometimes that worried her in quiet moments, although it seemed to be a common enough complaint among her contemporaries. There were plenty of good-time guys around, who would disappear like snow before the sun in times of trouble or if required to make a commitment.

That would most likely not be the case with Rupert Daniels, the unbidden thought came to her. He would be steadfast, she felt. Of course, she could be quite wrong— all she had to go on was a certain gut feeling. What an old-fashioned word that was—'steadfast'—yet very necessary in a relationship. Her mother had that quality, which had kept their family together. Not that she discounted her father's earning ability, which had been important throughout her childhood. No, she had no illusions there. Maybe Rupert would be steadfast, but he also had what could be a more than average estimation of his own desirability.

Leila thought of how rude she had been to him, which had been somewhat out of character for her. Although she could defend herself quite adequately when necessary at work, she stopped short of rudeness, brashness, sarcasm, behaviour she despised in others. How had she found the nerve to say that she didn't find him desirable? In spite of her chastening thoughts, she couldn't help grinning to herself at the memory of the expression on his face, a sort of controlled stupefaction. He had countered with the only response possible.

Her spirits lifted as she got into bed. What she had initiated had certainly cleared the air. On that comforting thought, she fell into a deep, exhausted sleep.

She woke up abruptly the next morning at ten minutes to six from force of habit, then realized that she could sleep in. As she stared at her bedside digital clock, she decided to telephone Stacey, who would be thinking of getting up to go to work.

'Hello,' her sister's voice said after two rings, sounding alert if not exactly chipper. 'Hello, Leila. I can seen it's you from my call-display unit. What's up?'

'Hi. Just felt like calling you. Won't keep you long. I'm on the evening shift myself,' Leila said quickly. 'Just wanted to let you know that I'm working with Dr Rupert Daniels, starting from yesterday. He's a new doc at our place.'

'Really?' Stacey said, a little guardedly. 'Well, that's a coincidence.'

'I, er, I'm not quite sure how to handle him,' she said. 'He knows I'm your sister. I felt a bit, sort of up-tight…you know.'

'Oh, well,' Stacey said, 'that's all water under the bridge now. I don't suppose it means anything to him whatsoever, so I don't think you have to take an attitude to it. I don't suppose there's anyone around Gresham General who knows or remembers. As for me, I've put it behind me. I must have been out of my mind to do what I did.'

'You mean you don't care any more?'

'No,' Stacey said, sounding a little weary. 'Thank heaven, I don't. Sometimes we do stupid things, trying to get what we want, when we have a deep need.'

'I'm glad you don't care,' Leila said.

'We were never lovers. Maybe I never told you that,' Stacey said. 'We went out a couple of times… He kissed me. I guess I gave him plenty of come-on. Is he giving you any sort of trouble?'

'No, not really,' Leila said. 'I just get the feeling that he's very wary of me, that's all.'

Stacey laughed. 'Contaminated by association?'

'Something like that.'

'Don't let him get away with that,' Stacey said. 'You can handle him, I'm sure. Anyway, why should it matter? It's not as though you want to have a relationship with him outside work, is it? You're always saying that you don't want to get involved with a doctor, and especially not an obstetrician.'

'No, of course not. It's just that working with him might be a bit awkward at first,' Leila said, somewhat cheered by her sister's pragmatism.

'Oh, just do your job to the best of your ability, be very professional and don't worry about anything else. I don't suppose he will. I heard rumours while I was in Gresham that he'd had a messy break-up with a woman, which might account for the way he is.'

'What way is that?' Leila asked.

'Standoffish,' Stacey said.

Biting back a ready retort that many men would be standoffish if they had been propositioned by Stacey, she merely said, 'Mmm.'

'Isn't he married?' Stacey said.

'It seems not, according to the internal telegraph. I can't say for certain,' Leila said.

'Got to go now, kid,' Stacey said. 'My toast has just popped up and my coffee's getting cold. Talk to you on the weekend. Tell him it's not catching if he goes on at you.'

Leila laughed. 'That's a thought,' she said. 'Talk to you later.'

The next two weeks of the evening shift went by very quickly. Several times Leila worked with Rupert, yet things were so hectic that all concentration was on the job in hand, with little time for personal conversation.

Both she and Anne were scheduled to have the weekend off at the end of their stint, then they would start the day shift on the Monday, back in rooms five and six in the obstetrics and gynaecology department.

At a quarter to midnight on the Friday, she and Anne were in the OR coffee-room for a sustaining cup of tea at the end of their last shift before heading home.

'What a night!' Anne said as she kicked off her shoes, plopped down in an armchair and put her feet up on the coffee-table, cradling a mug of hot tea in her hands.

'What can you expect on a Friday night?' Leila said, sitting down opposite her. 'People will drink too much, then drive. People will leave bad abdominal pain until a Friday evening before doing anything about it.'

'Yeah, that's human nature, I guess,' Anne said.

'Mmm, this tea's good,' Leila said, as she flexed her shoulder muscles. 'Makes me feel almost normal. I think every muscle in my body hurts from pushing and pulling those stretchers, yanking open those double doors every few minutes, heaving those huge packs about.'

'You love it,' Anne said. 'Admit it.'

'Yes, I guess I do. Wouldn't want to be anywhere else, except maybe the emergency department.'

'Ditto. We like the challenge, the drama, and the precision of it—right?'

The door of the coffee-room burst open just then, to admit Chuck Burney, closely followed by Rupert.

'Oh, damn,' Leila muttered. So far she hadn't completely mastered the art of sang-froid where he was concerned.

'Hi, guys,' Chuck. 'What's going on here?'

Anne perked up considerably at the sight of Chuck, on whom she had developed a very strong crush.

A little flustered, Leila swung her feet to the floor and stood up, noting as she did so that both doctors looked pale and exhausted. They had not been working in the OR that evening, so Leila assumed that they had been on the obstetrics floor, in the labour and delivery room.

'There's tea,' she said, 'in that pot. You're welcome to that. And there are cookies in the cupboard.'

'Thanks,' Chuck said.

'How are the twins that we delivered here a couple of weeks ago?' she asked, addressing herself to both doctors. 'The ones that were taken to Children's Hospital? I've been thinking a lot about them—can't get them off my mind.'

Rupert looked at her consideringly. 'They've been discharged from hospital and they're in the temporary foster-home now while we get the adoption under way,' he said. 'It shouldn't take long. They'll be going to their adoptive parents soon. So far they seem fine, in good health. They're really great kids.'

'I'm glad,' she said, still standing up, feeling a little awkward. 'Are you going to be in touch with the mother for some time?'

'Oh, yes,' he said, helping himself to tea. 'That will be an ongoing thing.' He seemed sober and serious. 'She wants the girl's second name to be Cathy, and I expect the adoptive parents will comply.'

'I hope so,' Leila murmured, thinking of the pale mother who could use some mothering herself.

'Bad parenting often runs in families, it seems to me,' Chuck said, managing to inject a light tone. 'I guess it comes from not having good examples to learn from.'

'Do you think that cycle can be broken?' Anne chipped in, smiling as Chuck plopped down beside her.

'Oh, I think it can be,' Chuck said thoughtfully, 'if a parent has a good mentor. Otherwise nothing would ever change, would it?'

'A healthy dose of cynicism helps,' Rupert said, and Leila looked at him sharply. 'When deciding what action to take.'

And you have plenty of that, I think, Leila wanted to say, but bit her tongue. She nodded, agreeing with what he had said in some ways, yet not wanting him to think that she was being sycophantic. She felt a little as though she were walking on eggshells with him, not even wanting to smile at him in case he took it the wrong way. Over the past days, Stacey's words had come back to her several times, about him having had a messy break with a woman in the past.

When she sat down again and Rupert sat near her, she looked straight ahead or down at her tea, her face impassive. 'Is the labour floor busy?' she asked. They had not had any Caesareans that evening.

'Hectic earlier on, everything happening at once,' Chuck said, 'so now it's pretty quiet.'

'All straightforward, normal,' Rupert said wearily. 'There's nothing else pending, so maybe we can actually get some sleep.'

'Sleep, what's that?' Chuck quipped. 'I couldn't tell you when I last had a good night's sleep.'

'Well, if you choose obstetrics as a specialty, Dr Burney, that's what you get,' Anne said. 'Or don't get.'

'Mmm,' he agreed. 'I'm determined that when I'm a staff man I'm only going to take on the numbers of patients I can handle comfortably, not like some guys who take on all comers and then wonder why they are working day and night.'

'Many of us have good intentions, Chuck,' Rupert said quietly.

'It's a good thing neither of us is married,' Chuck said artlessly, 'otherwise we'd be in the divorce stakes for sure.'

Leila held her breath for a few seconds as her thoughts flew to Stacey again. So he hadn't got somebody else on a permanent basis, hadn't spurned Stacey for somebody else...or so it seemed.

'Yeah, it's an occupational hazard,' Anne said brightly. 'Can I get you a mug of tea, Dr Burney?'

'Call me Chuck,' he invited. 'Yeah, tea would be great. I could use a bit of tender loving care, and having someone get you tea comes into that category.'

Anne got up, smiling, to oblige with the tea. Leila knew that she had been waiting for some time for Chuck to ask her out, but he never had. So far, she had hidden her adoration well under a veneer of sweet friendliness, which she extended to most people. If Chuck knew how she felt, he gave no overt indication of it.

'How about you, Rupert?' Chuck said, lounging back comfortably in his chair. 'Could you use a bit of tender loving care?'

Leila got slowly to her feet to pour herself more tea to hide her embarrassment.

'You could say that,' Rupert said thoughtfully, a hint of surprising laughter in his voice. 'What I need amounts to more than a cup of tea.'

Both Anne and Chuck laughed, while Leila busied herself pouring tea, her back to him, not feeling particularly amused. As she turned back to the room her eyes were drawn to Rupert inadvertently, to find him looking at her. She hadn't intended to make eye contact, and now the shock of his gaze, assessing and cynical, it seemed to her, albeit with a hint of amusement, left her nonplussed. Yet there was something else...a tension that she could not fathom, that she felt instinctively had nothing to do with Stacey.

For several seconds they looked at each other, while she wished that she were anywhere but there with him in the same room, hoping that Anne and Chuck would not notice anything amiss, any atmosphere between them, which could be the kiss of death for a good working relationship.

'But you have girlfriends, don't you?' Anne asked pertly. 'You're both normal guys.'

Chuck laughed. 'Nothing serious. I had one yesterday,' he said, 'but I haven't checked in with her today. That

could be a mistake. I just have to hope that I'm cute
enough that she'll hang in there.'

There was general laughter, in which Leila joined.

'As for Rupert here,' Chuck said, grinning, 'I happen
to know for sure that he has three on the go.'

'A fail-safe tactic, eh?' Anne laughed.

'You could say that,' Rupert said. For some reason
Leila felt there was a special message there for her, then
told herself not to be paranoid. 'You exaggerate, Chuck.'

'What about you, Leila?' Chuck asked with apparent
innocence, although Leila suspected that he was up to
something.

They were all looking at her. 'Nothing serious,' she
said, 'just a few tennis and squash friends.'

'What about you, Annie?' Chuck said, using her name
as an endearment, making her flush with pleasure. For all
his raw-boned, physical awkwardness, Chuck had a natural charm and knew how to play a woman like a violin,
Leila mused. Rupert, on the other hand, appeared to be
more subtle, and more devastating. Over the past two
weeks she had come to think of him as Rupert instead of
Dr Daniels, although she still strove for a professional
distance.

'I'm fancy-free at the moment,' Anne said, 'so I don't
have to worry.'

Fortunately, Anne began to chatter to Chuck about the
merits of working in different medical specialties in relation to marital satisfaction. They seemed not to notice
that Rupert was not saying anything, or that she, Leila,
stood with her back to the sink, sipping her tea, stiff with
tension. Her face felt tense with the effort of controlling
her emotions. So much for cool, she thought. If he had

not been so attractive, she didn't think she would care so much about his former relationship with Stacey.

One of the night nurses came in to get herself a cup of tea, breaking the tension. Leila took the opportunity to leave, with a quick, 'Goodnight.'

CHAPTER EIGHT

'MS HARDWICK, would you get the extra units of blood for me, please?'

The anaesthetist in room six addressed Leila, who was the circulating nurse.

'Yes,' she said.

It was a routine operating day for Rupert, a Wednesday in early October, and they were doing a hysterectomy on a woman who had early-stage uterine cancer.

As Leila went out to the corridor to get two units of blood, in plastic IV bags, from the cooling cupboard that was for the purpose, she considered the woman's history. Already somewhat anaemic from loss of blood prior to the operation, she was now losing more and the anaesthetist was making sure that her haemoglobin level was kept within normal range.

That morning they had had two cases involving in vitro fertilization—they had implanted fertilized ova into two women who had previously been infertile. They had done that in the other room in the suite. Now they were on their third case of the day, the hysterectomy in room six.

Leila opened the door of the blood-cooling cupboard and searched through the many plastic bags of blood there for those that bore the name of her patient. It was going to be a long day. They were just about on schedule, but if anything out of the ordinary happened, they would very soon be behind.

Back in the room, she and the anaesthetist checked the labels on the bags of blood with the patient's identification and the blood-work form that was in her chart to make sure that they had the right blood for the patient. When that had been done, she checked the necessary paperwork that had to be completed as the operation proceeded.

Then she let her mind wander back over the past few weeks. It was autumn now, and although she had worked a lot with Rupert, they had kept their relationship professional, albeit superficially friendly. After their late-night drink and conversation in the bar, she felt that she knew him better, but their relationship had not progressed in any way from there. That, she told herself, was the way she wanted it to be. Why, then, did she feel vaguely frustrated when he thanked her politely at the end of a working day for a great job she had done and wished her goodnight? Again and again she reminded herself that the last thing she wanted was to be singled out by an obstetrics man, to become in any way emotionally involved with one.

If she was honest with herself, which she sometimes tried not to be where he was concerned, she found him more attractive than was good for her, more so than any doctor she had worked with for a long time. The same applied to a lot of women who worked in the department, from her observations. Some flirted with him openly at work, behaviour which made her more determined not to emulate Stacey's behaviour in any way. His response to them was a friendly tolerance, managing to give the impression that if there was any choosing to be done, he would be the one to do it. He was definitely getting to her.

At the same time, she sensed that he found her attractive, too, yet was not willing to take any action on it. That reserve, and her resolve not to get involved with a doctor, formed a barrier between them. Sometimes she felt that barrier becoming more and more stressful. At the same time she felt a growing resentment about his condemnation of Stacey.

Although there was a sense that they knew where they stood with each other, there was also a sense of impasse in her, as though something between them ought to be moving forward...

For Rupert's part, he watched her frequently with that—it seemed to her—mildly cynical expression on his face that she found so irritating. At odd moments she would look up and find his eyes on her. Maybe he was thinking, in those moments, of the trouble he had had with her sister. No further mention had been made of Stacey. Leila sighed as quickly she brought her thoughts back to the here and now.

'Will this woman be all right?' she asked Rupert when he scrubbed out at the end of the case, while Chuck finished the final skin sutures. There was an overwhelming need in her, all of a sudden, to get a little personal attention from him, to have him look at her directly, speak to her. Not caring to analyse her feelings, she spoke to him first.

'There's every indication that she'll be all right,' he said, running a hand wearily over his face as though to brush away cobwebs. 'The tumour is small, confined to the uterus, no outside spread. I'm optimistic.'

'That's good,' she said, having been the one to talk to the patient as she had waited for her operation. 'She was very frightened.'

'Yes,' he said, looking at her full in the face. 'It's understandable. I'll talk to her as soon as she's out of the anaesthetic.' He threw his used surgical gown into the laundry bin. 'And how are you, Leila?' he added quietly.

'It seems like a long time since I've really spoken to you—since we were in that pub in the storm.'

The memory of that made her smile. 'Apart from being overworked, the usual occupational hazard, I'm all right,' she said, having the distinct feeling that he was going to ask her out for a drink, wondering how she would respond. That feeling gave her a moment of panic. Where he was concerned, her thoughts and emotions were jumbled, to say the least, as her attraction vied with her determination not to get involved.

The room telephone rang and the moment, inappropriate as it was, passed, leaving her feeling slightly dazed and winded, as though someone had punched her in the solar plexus.

'Is that Leila? This is Clara Nin,' the voice said.

'Yes, it's me, Dr Nin,' Leila said. 'What can I do for you?'

'Sorry to butt in during your operating list, but I left a file of patients' notes in the suture cupboard in room six when I was working there last night. Can you check for me that it's still there, and maybe arrange for someone to bring it to my office in the outpatient department? My room is the first inside the department.'

'Sure, Dr Nin. It is there. I'll bring it myself when I have a coffee- or lunch-break.'

'Thanks, Leila. If I'm not there in my office, please put it in the top drawer of the desk.'

'Will do.'

Rupert was leaving the room when she turned round. Working with him, she decided then, was becoming more of a strain with each passing week.

Their next two cases were laparoscopic tubal sterilizations, for which they used fibre-optic instruments that could be put into the abdominal cavity through a very tiny incision in the abdominal wall to show up the pelvic organs on a TV monitor. This was done for women who did not want any more children, although the procedure could sometimes be reversed if a woman changed her mind. Rupert clipped off each Fallopian tube with a small metal and silicone clip. It was all very neat, Leila decided, as she watched the procedure on the screen. She never failed to be impressed, although she had seen it done many times. Rupert was very slick.

'Time for lunch,' the relief nurse said as she came into the room to take over from one of the registered nurses so that they could go for lunch.

'You go, Leila,' Anne said. 'I'm not hungry yet.'

'OK.' Leila grinned at her colleague, suspecting that Anne wanted to wait until Chuck was having a coffee-break, so that she could join him in the coffee-room.

Normally, the surgeons and anaesthetists did not take lunch-breaks, but the nurses did—the former just made do with coffee and maybe a very quick snack of a muffin. Their schedule was so tight that they couldn't take the time for more. The operating list had to go on.

Taking Clara's file out of the cupboard, Leila went out quickly, put on her white lab coat over her scrub suit, some overshoes, and went out to the elevator to go down to the outpatient department.

There was no one in Clara's small office when Leila opened the door, having knocked. As she walked over to the desk, her attention was caught by several rather large framed photographs on the desk. There was one of Clara standing in a garden, holding two small dogs, long-haired dachshunds, and Leila smiled as she saw it, bending forward to have a closer look. There was another one of Clara with a man, whom Leila assumed was her husband. Then there was an older photograph of a group of six people, one of them being a considerably younger Clara and—her heart jumped as she recognized him—Rupert Daniels, with his arm around the shoulders of a young woman. They looked young and happy, medical students, standing in the grounds of what appeared to be the university, smiling at the camera.

On the wall above the desk was a large photograph of a medical school class, consisting of small individual head-and-shoulders photographs of the entire graduating class. With her curiosity piqued, Leila scanned the picture to find Clara, then Rupert, then the dark-haired, beautiful girl who was in the other picture. There she was, smiling out, her name printed in tiny letters under her picture—Ashlie Rayburn.

Again, her attention was drawn to the other casual photograph of the young Rupert with his arm around Ashlie Rayburn. They both looked so happy. That was the observation that immediately struck her, and to her horror she felt something like envy.

When her hand was on the desk drawer, about to put the file inside, the door opened and Clara entered.

'Hello, Leila,' she said. 'Is that the file? Thanks a lot for bringing it down. Things were hectic up there last night. I don't usually go around leaving patients' charts behind me.'

Feeling as though she had been caught invading the other woman's privacy, Leila smiled a little sheepishly. 'No problem.' She smiled back. 'I have to confess I've just been admiring your photographs, especially the one with the dogs.'

'Aren't they sweet? I call then Null and Void,' Clara said.

'Oh, you don't!' Leila laughed.

'Do.' Clara came forward, pointing at the larger desk

photograph. 'And that's me in my youth, the last year in medical school. It seems like a thousand years ago, believe me. That's Rupert Daniels, in case you didn't recognize him.'

'He...he looks very happy,' Leila commented.

'So you've noticed that now he doesn't look happy?' Clara said, looking at her speculatively.

'Well...' she said.

'Don't be coy, Leila. You wouldn't be the first woman to realize he's got something bothering him,' Clara said, somewhat brusquely. 'He had a thing with the very beautiful Ashlie Rayburn, whom you see there in the picture. It didn't end well. I don't like to gossip, so I won't, but if you need to know about it any time, I'll tell you. I know you'll keep a confidence.'

'Need to know?' Leila said, her cheeks flushing.

'A lot of women find Rupert attractive,' Clara went on relentlessly. 'I sense that you do, too.'

'Oh, no!' Leila burst out. 'Is it obvious?'

'No, it isn't obvious. I'm just good at spotting the manifestations of underlying emotion. I need that for my job if I'm to be any good,' Clara said with equanimity, smiling at her own lack of modesty. 'I know I'm insufferable sometimes, pompous and all that. Rupert's a great guy in every way, great for the right woman. He just likes to be very, very careful. Enough said. I'm very fond of Rupert.'

'I...' Leila said.

'You would be good for him.'

'Me?' Leila said, incredulous, her cheeks hot now. 'He scarcely knows I exist as a woman.'

'I wouldn't be so sure. It would really be better if he were to tell you himself, rather than me telling you,' Clara said. 'I suggest that you get him to ask you out.'

'Oh, I wouldn't know how to do that,' Leila protested.

'Of course you would,' Clara said impatiently. 'Go to it. Women have been doing that since time immemorial, making the man think that the suggestion came from him.'

'Sounds devious,' Leila commented.

'Not devious—subtle,' Clara countered.

When someone knocked on the door, Leila left, hurried along the outpatient corridor to the elevator back to the OR. Obviously Clara did not know anything about Stacey and her play for Rupert, otherwise she would most likely not have said what she had. Was she match-making? What a very peculiar situation.

There was only time for her to eat a sandwich, very quickly, in the coffee-room, which she did standing up, washing it down with a glass of water, before she headed back to room six. So much for a lunch-break.

The relief nurse was still there, would stay there while Anne took her lunch-break.

'Hey, Leila.' Anne took her arm as she came inside, as they were changing from one case to the next. 'Guess what?'

'I'm no good at guessing,' she said. Anne looked excited and happy.

'Chuck's asked me out for a drink on the weekend,' Anne said, keeping her voice down. 'I thought it was never going to happen. Keep it quiet. Don't want any gossip.'

'That's great,' Leila whispered back. 'He's a super guy.'

As Anne went out, Leila felt an uncharacteristic sobering sadness, disturbed as she was by Clara's blunt remarks and suggestions that she would be good for Rupert. So many other people in her age group were getting into relationships, yet something meaningful eluded her, when most of the men she met were the ones she had hoped to avoid getting serious about. What a strange thing to say, she thought now, as though Clara had been pushing her into taking the initiative. There was no way that she wanted to take that initiative. Rupert wasn't right for her, and if he had been right for her, there was no way she could take the initiative with Stacey in the background. She supposed there wasn't a snowball's chance in hell that he would want her, even though he was attracted to her, it seemed.

Restlessly, she went about her work, preparing for the next case in room six, trying unsuccessfully to empty her mind of all thoughts related to Clara's revelations.

It was a relief when the working day came to an end. It had been stressful and hectic, an effort to keep on schedule. Leila felt drained as she made her way to the coffee-room for a quick cup of tea before changing to go home. She almost didn't go in when she saw that Rupert and Chuck were there, having the idea that her awareness of Rupert as an attractive man might be obvious to all and sundry. Anne was there, too, looking radiantly happy for someone who had just endured a very rushed day.

'Hi,' Anne accosted her. 'Dr Daniels has just asked us if we'd like to come to the baptism of those gorgeous twins that we all helped to deliver some weeks back, the ones who've been adopted.'

'Oh... Am I invited?' She looked directly at Rupert.

'Yes, if you'd like to come,' he said quietly, standing near her, looking very attractive divested of his paper hat and mask, his thick, dark hair untidy. 'The adoptive parents have asked me to be the godfather, so I have to go.'

'So you accepted?' she said.

'Yes.' He grimaced wryly. 'It's big responsibility, of which I've had no prior experience.'

'You could say that of parenthood,' she said.

'True. I thought maybe all of you who were here that evening when the babies were delivered would like to see how they've grown,' he said, 'as well as see them with their new parents. They adore them.'

'I'd love to come,' she said truthfully.

'It's this coming Sunday, early afternoon,' he said. 'Then I thought you could all come to my place for a late lunch or early supper afterwards, if you would like to.'

'We'd like that,' Anne chipped in. 'It's not often we get a chance to see "our" babies, or get invited to supper by an obstetrician.'

'How about if we all go for a quick drink right now?' Rupert countered. 'Over at the Captain's Arms?' He referred to a pub, modelled on the lines of an Irish pub, on a side street opposite the hospital emergency department that was a favourite hangout for staff, especially the junior staff. 'It will be my treat. I want to say thank you all for being such a great team, for helping me to settle into this hospital. I'll get Greg as well.'

'We'd love to!' Anne said quickly, speaking for everyone else.

'Right,' he said. 'I'll meet you over there in, say, twenty minutes?'

'Great!' Anne said again, while Leila simply opened and closed her mouth.

'With you around,' she said to Anne when the men had left, 'one doesn't have to be subtle.'

'What are you talking about? He wasn't subtle. I know you like him, Leila, so don't come on all high and mighty, per-lease,' Anne said. 'Come on, let's get changed pronto.'

'Yes, I do like him,' she admitted as they walked to the locker room, 'but I have reasons for not letting him know it. I'll tell you about it some time.' For a short while she would be thrown together socially with Rupert, yet in the company of others, where there was safety in numbers.

'He's a great guy,' Anne commented. 'If I wasn't so enamoured of Chuck, I could go for him in a big way.'

'I wouldn't want to join the queue,' Leila said. 'Why would he be seriously interested in me?'

'You sell yourself short,' Anne said bluntly.

'Maybe,' Leila murmured. 'I'm glad about the invitation to the baptism. I'd certainly love to see those babies.'

'He's going to give us all the information about how to get to the church, and his place later in the week,' Anne said.

All in all, it had been a somewhat unusual day.

The two bars of the Captain's Arms were crowded when they entered, even though it was early evening. A cool, blustery wind, and an early darkness that presaged winter, had driven many people inside, and Leila recognized a number of the young doctors from the hospital.

Chuck and Rupert materialized from the crowd when she and Anne entered. 'We've found a table at the back,' Chuck said, 'if you can fight your way back to it.' He disappeared with Anne into the thick of the crowd, leaving Leila with Rupert.

'Come with me to the bar,' he said, putting an arm protectively around her shoulders, easing her with him through the crush. 'What would you like to drink?'

'I wonder why it's so crowded,' she said, very aware of his arm around her, his body touching hers as other people pressed against them.

'There's a wedding reception in an upstairs room,' he said. 'It looks as though there's an overspill down here.'

'Yes.' For the first time she noticed men in dinner jackets and women wearing dressy outfits with flowers pinned to the fronts. 'A lot of champagne has been going around, I think.' It was all such a sudden contrast from the work setting that she found herself smiling with excitement, enjoying the presence of her companion. Clara's words came back to her about being subtle.

'Ouch!' Someone pushed her from the back and she found herself standing with her face pressed against Rupert's chest. 'Sorry.'

'What?' he said, bending down to her. 'Would you like some champagne?'

'No…lager's fine,' she said. With his face so close to her own, she found herself staring up into his eyes, while some members of the wedding party started to sing a rousing, sentimental song. She and Rupert were wedged inside a noisy mass of people.

'What?' he said.

'Lager,' she mouthed the word.

Then, without knowing quite how it happened, his mouth, so close, touched hers. No one around them took the slightest notice when he put both his arms round her and kissed her properly, the touch of his mouth sending shock waves through her. Before she could do anything, he pulled away, his hand sliding down her arm to grasp her hand and pull her after him to the bar, fighting for a space.

'Two lagers, please,' he ordered, easing her up beside him. In a state of shock, Leila said nothing, her lips hypersensitive and tingling from his touch.

'There's no point in trying to fight our way back to the table,' he shouted in her ear. 'I can't stay long. If my pager goes off, I'll never hear it in this noise.'

Leila nodded. More than anything, she wanted him to kiss her again. To him it probably had not meant anything, prompted as it had been by their close proximity, so she must not read too much into it, she told herself desperately as she felt herself softening towards him in a dangerous way.

Conversation was impossible, so they sipped their drinks side by side, having moved along the bar a little to a slightly quieter spot. There was no sign of Chuck, Greg and Anne. Ruefully, Rupert grinned at her and shrugged, a certain light of awareness in his eyes, it seemed to her, that had not been there before. The odd feeling came to her that he was perhaps testing her in some way, and she didn't know what to do.

They parted later in the hospital parking lot. Rupert's pager had gone off as they had walked the short distance back to the hospital. A light drizzle was falling, to add to the cooler temperature. Falling leaves blew around them from the big maple trees that grew beside the street.

'I like autumn,' Leila said. 'It's my favourite season. I like the mellowness of it.'

'It's mine, too,' he said, as they stopped in the parking lot. Again his pager beeped imperiously and he reached into his pocket to switch it off, after checking the call-display. 'Will you come on Sunday?'

'Yes, I'd like to,' she said sincerely. 'Why did you kiss me?'

'I thought it was mutual,' he said. 'There you were, so tantalizingly in front of me. Leila, I'm sorry, but I really must go.'

He left her, striding out quickly for the main entrance.

Leila didn't sleep well that night, tossing and turning, with the memory of Rupert's kiss on her mind, wondering what it meant...if anything.

CHAPTER NINE

SUNDAY was wet and cool, a typical late autumn day, with the scent of fallen leaves and soil moistened by rain strong in the air, the sort of day that Leila loved.

When she went for a walk at nine o'clock in the morning there were few other people about in her residential area. Warmly dressed in raincoat, scarf and hat, sheltered under her umbrella, she strode out, revelling in the moisture-laden air which gave her skin a healthy glow, in spite of a certain city pollution that was always there. In the cooler weather it was not too obvious.

She had arranged to be picked up by Chuck and Anne in Chuck's car to go to the baptism later, as her own car was playing up again. Although her father had offered to buy her a new car, she had declined, wanting to pay her own way on that, as her parents were already helping her with the house. Yesterday she had visited her parents, surprised to find her father at home, enjoying lunch with her mother.

'Have you said something to him, Leila?' her mother had whispered to her in the kitchen, while her father had been reading a newspaper in the sitting room. 'Your father's been home a lot lately at weekends and evenings. I don't know whether it's because his work is finally tailing off, or whether he's really decided to spend more time on other things. It seems like too much to hope for.'

'Well, I did suggest a few weeks ago that he should spend more time away from the hospital because he was interfering with what a new doctor was doing in the department,' Leila had said as she'd helped her mother. 'I didn't hold out much hope that he would listen to me, but it's great that he seems to have taken the hint.'

'We're going to a concert and a play this coming week,' her had mother said, 'and out to dinner first before each one. I can hardly believe it's happening.'

'Don't knock it, Mum,' Leila whispered.

'Oh, I won't,' her mother said. 'I'm going to plan a winter holiday, to somewhere hot, while he's in this mood.'

'It's absolutely great,' Leila said, giving her mother a bear hug and a kiss. 'Long may it last.' Then she went on to tell her mother about the baptism, the babies who had been adopted, then, hesitantly, about Rupert Daniels.

'The very same who had all that trouble...you know...with Stacey?' her mother said, with something like awe in her voice.

'The very same,' Leila said.

'That must have been a bit tricky for you,' her mother commented, giving her a shrewd look, stopping what she was doing to serve up the delicious light lunch she had prepared. 'Why didn't you tell me about him before?'

'Didn't want to worry you. It *was* a bit tricky at first, but it seems to be better now,' she said, glossing over the angst she had experienced, the strange standoff that she and Rupert seemed to be in now, like two wary animals circling each other, not having made up their minds whether to fight or to retreat. All of which had little to do with her sister.

Whatever it was that had been in his past with Ashlie Rayburn, Leila sensed the angst of it in him. Time and time again, she told herself that it had nothing to do with her, yet when she saw Rupert watching her, looking at her when he thought she would not be aware of his scrutiny, she felt the tension increasing in her to an unbearable degree, and she was not sure why except that she was becoming more and more attracted to him. 'Join the queue,' she told herself ruefully many times as she watched other women in the department make a play for him. Keeping her distance was a matter of principle and integrity with her.

'I should hope so,' her mother said, not deceived. 'Your job's stressful enough without having that heaped on top of it. Stressful for him, too, I expect. Do you like him?' She seemed to be picking up vibes.

'Oh, I don't dislike him,' Leila said, keeping her voice casual. 'Heaven forbid that I should ever get involved in any way with an obstetrician.'

'Most of the young ones have a different attitude, from what I've seen of them,' her mother said, giving her a wry grin. 'They don't want to be on call twenty-four hours a day, seven days a week. Whether that's better for the patients or not, I haven't decided yet. It must be better to have a more relaxed, well-rounded person dealing with things.'

Leila dearly wanted to tell her mother what she was feeling about Rupert, but she didn't really know herself, it was all so…nebulous.

As she walked now on Sunday, in the rain, she felt that somehow the day was significant. Going to the baptism with him was somehow like having a date with Rupert, a group date. She smiled ruefully to herself. Was that what she wanted? A date with him? And what would she say if he actually asked her out?

Pushing it from her mind as much as she could, she concentrated on the scene around her, the russet leaves on the sidewalk, darkened with rain, the bare trees, gardens dying down for the winter.

After a light lunch, she got ready to go to the church, dressing with care. Not today the blue jeans with water stains around the ankles. She put on a long, soft wool skirt in a pale grey colour, shoes with a thick two-inch heel and a thin cashmere sweater in a beautiful purple colour that complemented the skirt and did wonders for her pale face and hair, and her eyes. She would wear boots to the church, take her shoes in a bag to wear at Rupert's house.

Her hair was newly washed, shiny and soft, with wisps curling around her face, unlike the bedraggled mop it had been when Rupert had taken her to the bar. She wanted him to see that she could be sophisticated. Carefully she applied delicate make-up, with a smoky blue eye-shadow that gave depth to her eyes.

When the telephone rang moments later it was Anne. 'Hi,' she said breathlessly. 'We're leaving now to come to get you.'

'Great! I'm ready,' Leila said, feeling a churning in her breast, a sudden nervousness, at the thought of meeting Rupert out of the usual context.

Don't be ridiculous, she told herself as she put on a long wool coat, a scarf and hat. It's going to be all right.

Outside a gentle rain fell as she waited under the small porch roof for Chuck and Anne.

There were quite a lot of people for the baptism at the church when they arrived, with many more leaving. Obviously a service had just ended. As Chuck, Anne and Leila made their way to the front of the cavernous church, Leila recognized several social workers with whom she had had dealings at the hospital, all dressed smartly, grouped in the area by the font. There were several other nurses, too, from the neonatal intensive care unit and the labour floor of the hospital, as well as some doctors from various departments. Clara Nin was there, too.

The minister appeared from the nether regions of the church, together with a youngish couple holding the babies, Rupert and an unknown older woman, whom Leila took to be the adoptive grandmother or maybe the god-mother. Seeing Rupert, she hung back. He looked dev-astatingly attractive in an immaculate dark grey suit with a dark blue shirt. As she looked at him, so he looked over and saw her as she brought up the rear of her little party, acknowledging her presence with a slight nod and smile.

'The babies are quiet,' Chuck commented. 'Whenever I've been to one of these events, which isn't very often, the kids have been bawling.' Chuck looked suave in a neat black suit, white shirt and red tie.

'There's still time,' Anne said.

The ceremony got under way very quickly, with the babies being passed around to the principle players in what seemed to Leila like a tableau. As Rupert held one of the babies, she found that she could scarcely look at him, yet her eyes were drawn back to him again and again. He looked so natural, competent, gentle...and right, holding a baby. After all, that was his job, she reminded herself. He also looked relaxed and happy.

The babies were to be named Aiysha Catherine and Alexander, the word spread around as the minister applied the holy water, touching the forehead of each child with it. Still they slept on placidly. Someone made a joke that Leila could not hear fully, and Rupert smiled.

In that moment Leila knew that she was in love with Rupert Daniels. The knowledge came to her with a clear certainty, as though someone had spoken the fact inside her head, brooking no denial. The awful thing that she had been guarding against had happened, the unwelcome involvement. As she stared, as though mesmerized, at Rupert, Stacey's voice seemed to come out of the past again and haunt her: 'I've met this gorgeous man...' Then she was reminded of his comment: 'I'm not on offer.'

With the same rare clarity, she understood at an emotional level that she wanted love from a mature man, an intelligent, sophisticated man, someone she could love in return. Up to now, the men she had been fraternizing with either seemed like mere boys or lacked that extra something that captivated a lasting interest and emotion.

A flush suffused her whole body, of which not much was visible, thank goodness, she thought desperately. She felt a little sick, as though she might faint. Swallowing nervously, she lowered her head and looked around surreptitiously for ways of escape.

There were none. The church had emptied of all but their party. She was wedged between Chuck and an elderly man as they all stood in a tight semicircle around the font. Also, it was an awfully long way to the main door.

When the ceremony was over, they all got to look at the babies, who were beautifully dressed in traditional long white gowns and wrapped in soft wool shawls to keep them warm against the autumn chill.

'Satisfied, Leila?' a voice said softly behind her shoulder as she leaned forward to look at the babies, who were as beautiful as their clothing, looking healthy and plump, their skin dewy. 'I know you were concerned about them.'

Rupert stood next to her, looking down at her perceptively, so close that she had a strong desire to reach out and touch his dark hair where it curled up over his collar at the back. 'Yes, I am,' she replied quietly, breaking away from the small knot of people around the couple who were holding the babies. 'Although I...I can't help thinking about the mother...that young girl.'

Images of the pale girl on the operating table came back to Leila again, Cathy's straggly hair covered by one of the blue paper mob-caps that the patients wore, not totally covering it, which had made her look vulnerable and pathetic.

In her mind's eye she saw again the little-girl hands, with the uncared-for fingernails, with intravenous lines piercing the delicate blue veins in the backs of them. There had been something about those hands, quiescent under the anaesthetic, that had touched her deeply at the time, as had the dark lashes of the closed eyes touching the cheeks, the eyes of a child in sleep. Those hands would not hold those beautiful babies that she had produced.

Had that girl ever been loved by anyone? Had there been love that would have given her some of the necessary emotional strength to cope with motherhood and her own life, whatever it might bring?

Leila realized then that she was staring back fixedly at Rupert while those images renewed themselves in her mind, and she felt immensely sober, to such a degree that her eyes moistened with tears. Even the reality of the happy adoptive parents—ecstatic would be a better word, she thought—and the cherished babies could not diminish the clarity of the images of the child-mother.

'I know. I think about the mother, too,' he said quietly, taking her arm and leading her away towards the rows of pews. 'I'm in touch with her, and will be for some time, I imagine. She's still my patient. The adoptive parents have agreed that I should show her photographs of the babies from time to time if she asks to see them.'

'I understand that she's reserved the right to see the babies sometimes if she wants to?' Leila said.

'Yes,' he said. 'Although she sometimes professes indifference, I know that it's not total. That has a lot to do with her circumstances. Maybe when she's older she'll want to know more. In the meantime, this is the very best solution for the kids, don't you think?'

'Yes, one has to admit that it is. All the family here adores them, it's very obvious. They're very lucky, and they know it. There aren't too many babies available now,' Leila said, more disturbed by his attractive presence than she knew how to cope with, and the strain of trying not to show it.

'You sound envious,' he said, his eyes probing her slightly flushed features. 'Are you?'

'I am...I think,' she said. At that moment, struggling with a welter of emotion, she was not sure that envy fitted into the spectrum. 'That's...um, not characteristic of me. Usually I don't envy anyone. I generally assume that what other people have that is enviable, I can get for myself if I really want to.'

'Has that hypothesis been tested very often?' he asked lightly.

'Not in anything as complicated as having twins,' she admitted, breaking into a smile at his attentive interest that held a hint of mockery in it. 'I could be out of my depth there.'

'Mmm,' he said. Their eyes locked, and she found that she could not look away, held in the emotion of all that was left unspoken, remembering his kiss which had been light-hearted, almost inconsequential. If only she could ask him about Ashlie Rayburn...

'Even if the mother chooses not to keep in touch, in these relatively enlightened days,' he said, his gaze mov-

ing to her mouth, then roving over her features, 'the kids
will be able to trace their mother later on, if she still wants
to be traced, now that adoption isn't a closed book any
more.'

Leila swallowed nervously once more, falling into step
with him as he strolled towards the church door. 'Yes,'
she said. His arm, brushing against hers, sent shivers of
sensitivity through her. It was becoming clearer to her
why he was doing the job he was doing, in the way that
he was doing it.

She had never been aware that her father, and some of
the other obstetricians, experienced a great deal of angst
over the world in which they worked. Some were sensitive
and thoughtful, while many others seemed to let everything wash over them, to distance themselves from the
social circumstances of their patients. Some of them even
seemed to operate in a sort of never-never land of denial,
pretending that everything in the garden was lovely.

'Are you coming to my place for some food?' Rupert
asked.

'Yes, please.'

'Are you driving?'

'I came with Chuck and Anne,' she said. 'They'll give
me a ride. My car's playing up again.'

'See you there, then,' he said, as other people came up
to them, taking him away from her, giving her a sharp,
odd sense of loss.

Clara came up and linked her arm through his. 'Come
on, Rupert,' she said. 'Come and do your host bit.' She
winked at Leila. 'I must say that you looked absolutely
divine as a godfather, very suave. It becomes you.'

Dazedly, Leila joined Chuck and Anne, trailing behind
the others out of the church. As they came out into the
air, to be met by a light drizzle, all she could think of

were comforting clichés to cover the situation—'funny old world' and 'all's well that ends well'. Although it was wonderful and uplifting to see those babies in an obviously very loving and secure family, the other side of the coin, the hidden side, was still there.

As for her feelings for Rupert, there were no clichés for those. They were as tempestuous as a summer thunderstorm, and as unpredictable. Hadn't she wanted something tempestuous? She remembered using that word to Anne. But she had meant it in the context of a mutual love. In this situation, she very much doubted that it would be mutual. Although he had been friendly to her, and polite, and was no doubt sexually attracted to her, she remembered his coldness when he had said, 'I'm not on offer.'

'What a lovely house!' She was the first to voice an opinion about Rupert's house as they all got out of the car in his street, determined as she was to keep her emotions to herself, to elevate her own mood. No doubt Rupert would be serving wine and she was looking forward to having a glass of it.

They were in a small residential cul-de-sac, not far from the downtown of Gresham, in an old established residential area, with lots of mature trees and shrubs around, now largely the russet, yellow and red of autumn.

They stood on the street in front of the house and stared up at the charming building which was made of mellow red brick and stone, that looked as though it had been built in the mid-to-late 1800's, really old by Ontario standards. A well-tended garden of small terraces and rock gardens separated the house from the street.

'Yeah,' Chuck agreed. 'Rupert has good taste in just about everything he does.'

That remark gave Leila a sobering, chill feeling, and

something close to depression settled on her as they
mounted the few steps from the street and walked along
a stone path to the front door. His good taste had not
extended to Stacey, she thought. By association, it would
not extend to her either, she assumed. Maybe she was
being masochistic to come here, to have any dealings with
Rupert outside work.

CHAPTER TEN

RUPERT met them at the door. 'Hi,' he said, smiling. 'Glad you could all make it. I just got here myself.' He had had time to change into a pair of casual green cords and a grey sweater, which made him look no less attractive than the more formal attire.

Leila looked him over quickly, then looked away again. No doubt Anne and Chuck would soon tune in to her mood if she wasn't careful. There seemed to be a hopelessness about her emotional involvement with Rupert that contrasted with what seemed to her the mutual attraction of Chuck and Anne, which seemed to be blossoming in a far less complicated way.

'Come into the dining room and get something to eat when you're ready,' he said. 'It's every man for himself, and every woman for herself. You can leave your coats upstairs, first room on the right.'

Leila unzipped her leather boots, left them with other boots in the vast hallway, then slipped into her shoes.

'Glad you could come, Leila,' Rupert said to her quietly, when she was the first one to come back down the stairs. 'I had a feeling you might chicken out.'

She hid a smile when she saw him looking her over like a man who might have looked at a horse he wanted to buy at a country fair, now that she was divested of her coat. The imagery did something positive for her mood.

'My curiosity was piqued,' she said. 'Show me a man's books and pictures and I'll know the man. Something like that.'

'Look as much as you want,' he said, smiling. He put a hand under her elbow. 'This way.'

Very conscious of his touch, she resisted the urge to pull away. She wondered why he seemed to be going out of his way to be pleasant to her when he would perhaps have preferred to ignore her. Perhaps he wanted to show that he could, after all, be magnanimous. Nonetheless, she wanted to scream at him, Don't be nice to me if you don't mean it, if it doesn't mean anything to you, because I can't bear it. And above all, don't touch me!

Instead, she remained mute, suffering his touch, outwardly serene...or so she hoped.

'Did you cook?' she asked, looking at the delicious array of food spread out on a large dining table.

'No,' he said, smiling. 'I have a housekeeper who kindly agreed to come in today to get this ready. Her name's Albertina, she's Portuguese, very good with fish and shellfish. I have to clear up, though. And I can cook,' he added, 'in case you're thinking what a useless guy I must be around the home. My interns are coming as well. I thought I might take advantage of the occasion to broaden the scope, since I don't get to entertain much.'

'Great idea.' Leila was about to say that he didn't have anyone to benefit from his skills, but bit her tongue just in time—he might think that she would propose marriage next. There was a tension in him, as there was in her, as they talked.

'Is everything all right?' Rupert said suddenly, still standing beside her. 'You looked worried then, and sort of tuned out on me.'

'What? Oh... No, I...' she began. 'What I mean is...yes, I'm all right. Could I, please, have a glass of that white wine you have there? I'm just dying for a drink.'

'Sure.' He took her over to a massive antique sideboard

where several open bottles of white wine, were languishing in ice coolers. There were also several bottles of red wine. Some had already been poured.

The doorbell rang and moments later the hall was filled with other hospital staff, some of whom had been at the church, including Clara, while others were the interns from the hospital who worked with Rupert, including Greg Amos.

Armed with a glass of white wine, Leila surveyed the scene, glad to see Greg. Maybe, after all, she was going to enjoy this interlude.

'I'm going to enjoy this,' Anne said, *sotto voce*, to Leila. 'Super food, super wine, and super company.' Anne looked very pretty and sophisticated in black velvet pants, close-fitting, and a sleeveless red velvet top. Leila noted that Chuck was either staying close to Anne or was looking at her.

They carried their food into a sitting room, which was huge, filled tastefully with antique furniture and comfortable sofas and chairs. There were two sets of French doors leading out to a terrace at the back of the house. When Greg came over to talk to her, Leila knew that it was going to be all right. There were enough people to act as a buffer between herself and Rupert so she wouldn't make a fool of herself by letting him see how she felt.

The next two hours went by in a pleasant haze of wine, good food and conversation, with no more direct interaction with Rupert until someone put on some music and one or two people started to dance, slowly and lazily.

'Do you dance?' Rupert asked her, suddenly there beside her again.

Dumbly, she nodded, putting down her wineglass and moving into his arms, sensing that he was merely being polite. As she did so, she caught the glance of Clara, whose expression was enigmatic, reminding Leila of what she had said in her office—that she would tell her about Rupert if there was anything she wanted to know. Not sure what Clara had meant at the time, she was no more sure now as Rupert took her hand warmly and slid the other arm round her waist, easing her close to him as a slow, seductive tune filled the room, blotting out all conversation, which had become loud over the course of the afternoon. Stiffly, she moved in the circle of his arms. The room was pleasantly dim as the late autumn gloom closed in outside, and no one had put lights on in the room yet. A light from the hallway filtered in, giving a soft yellow glow.

'I won't bite,' he said.

'I'm not so sure,' she countered. 'I suspect you could do worse than bite.'

He bent his head so that his mouth was close to her ear. 'Enjoy yourself, Leila,' he murmured. 'I am.' With that, he kissed her ear, gently brushing it with his lips, so that she felt her knees go weak as a sudden flush of intense need enveloped her, making her close her eyes and involuntarily sway towards him.

'Let yourself go,' he said, his head close to hers.

'Why should I let myself go,' she said, gathering her reserves, 'when I know that's the last thing you'll be doing…with me?' It took all her will-power not to turn her head the short distance so that his mouth, so close to her ear, would meet her lips. A familiar, hysterical desire to laugh welled up in her. Too much wine, she told herself muzzily, although she had only had two glasses, small ones at that.

'You've grown on me, Leila Hardwick,' he said, steering her out of a crush of dancers now that almost everyone was on the floor, shuffling over the beautiful oriental carpet.

'You're kidding,' she said.

'No, I'm not.'

'Don't get too used to it, then,' she said, her voice husky. 'It's bound to be short-lived.'

When he laughed, more of a sexy chuckle, she felt that if she were not careful she would be the proverbial putty in his hands, and before she knew it she could be following in the footsteps of her sister, making an utter fool of herself, only to be coldly rebuffed by him.

'Don't be so sure,' he said.

'Just because almost every woman and her dog are chasing you at work, you don't have to make assumptions,' she said haughtily, drawing back her head and looking at him down her nose. 'Assumptions that you're irresistible.' And he would be so right, she thought.

At that, he grinned at her slowly and lazily in a very irritating way.

After dancing with him for some time, becoming more and more sensitized to his presence, he suddenly got called away to the telephone. At the same time the pagers of some of the interns started to beep, although they were not the ones on call. Perhaps there was an emergency in which more hands were needed, Leila surmised. Quickly, a few people prepared to leave.

Leila, feeling bereft, went out to the terrace through one of the French doors that had been left slightly open, feeling in need of some fresh air. It had been a lovely afternoon, relaxed and pleasant in this sophisticated house that managed to be very welcoming also, so much so that she could happily have stayed there for the evening.

The early evening was crisp, pleasantly cool, with the scent of fallen leaves and soil coming from the garden.

That garden disappeared into the near distance from the terrace. Leila walked down a few stone steps from the terrace onto a path, then stopped to take deep breaths. Beyond the end of the garden would be a ravine, she surmised, as Gresham was liberally endowed by nature with these natural parks where wildlife still flourished, places that had never been practicable for building. Now they provided green oases for the city, lungs as it were, in the pollution of traffic fumes.

She walked down the path, needing to think.

'What the hell am I doing here?' she whispered to herself. What she wanted was a deep mutual love, not to be in love with someone who could take his pick from a large number of available women, albeit a man who had a quiet integrity and charismatic quality that was extremely difficult for any woman to resist. At work she had witnessed the most ardent man-haters, of all ages, turn to jelly under his attentions.

Time was marching on, bringing with it a sharp sense of angst, the like of which she had not experienced before, a feeling that was bitter-sweet, mingling as it did with the pain in the region of her heart, a feeling that she recognized instinctively as the pain of love. Always she seemed to be in a process of becoming, never arriving. Perhaps it was like that for most people, she mused, even the ones who seemed to have what they wanted.

Abruptly she turned on her heel and walked back to the house. It would soon be time to go as the party was breaking up. Inside the house she walked up a back staircase and found a bathroom on the next floor, where she dabbed cool water on her flushed cheeks, then added a little make-up, taking her time.

As she walked slowly back down, she was aware that the music had been turned off, that there was quiet where there had been the loud buzz of conversation. The sitting room was empty. She wandered through to the dining room, which was also empty.

'Leila!' Rupert was calling her from the main hall.

'I'm here,' she said, going out to him. 'Where is everybody?'

'A few people got called out,' he replied, coming towards her, 'both for the operating room and for the labour floor. Things are hectic there. The others decided to leave, too.'

'You have to go?' she asked.

'No.'

'Where are Chuck and Anne?' she asked, looking around. 'They have to give me a ride home.'

'They also left,' he said. 'I think they wanted to be alone.'

'But...' She was breathing quickly, having difficulty getting her breath.

'I'll take you home,' he said.

'Oh, you don't have to,' she said.

'We've had this conversation before,' he said. 'I do have to. There are some buses from near here, but they're few and far between.' He came to her and put his hands on her upper arms. 'Leila...I want to talk to you.'

'Don't.' She pulled back from him. There seemed to be no one in the house now but the two of them, and she was frightened of what she might do, of how she might let herself go with him, behave like an idiot...

She turned and walked back blindly into the sitting room, where a log fire burned in a substantial grate, providing the only light in the room. Irresolutely, she stopped in front of it. She felt like a moth blundering about, having been confronted with a brilliant light after being released from a dark room.

Sensing that Rupert had come in behind her, she tensed.

'Leila...' he said.

'Don't come near me,' she said, turning round to him, her back to the fire. 'Don't touch me.'

'I wasn't going to touch you,' he said, standing near her. 'Leila, what is it?'

'I don't want you accusing me of being like my sister,' she said wildly, knowing that she was being irrational, was probably destroying the rapport that they had built up over the past weeks. Oh, God! Couldn't he see that she was in love with him, that she was crying inside for something that did not have a snowball's chance in hell of ever coming to fruition? Perversely, there was no way that she wanted him to know it.

'I want to talk to you about your father,' he said gently.

'My father?'

'Come and sit down,' he said. 'I want your input about an idea that I have.' He put out a hand to her and she took a step back, feeling the heat of the fire.

When he sat down in a chair, she slowly followed, sitting away from him but facing him. Somehow she felt that she was going mad. Was that what love did to you? That all-consuming feeling that you no longer had control of your emotions, or your life? It was the fact of being alone with him, she realized, without the familiar buffer of work and numerous colleagues between them. If he touched her again she would be totally lost.

'To get right to the point,' he said, 'there are times at work when I need another assistant surgeon, someone experienced preferably, when the residents and interns are either not available or have already been grossly overworked and need to rest. I've been thinking for some time that your father might be willing to take the job...it would be an occasional job. What do you think?'

Leila sat twisting her hands together in her lap, looking down at them then back at him. This was unexpected, and she strove to wrench her thoughts back from a different plane, her emotions churning as she felt on the edge of disintegration.

'I...' She licked her dry lips. 'I expect he would be happy to do that, approached in the right way,' she managed to get out. 'But I'm not sure my mother would. She's trying to wean him away from the hospital.'

'This might actually work in her favour,' he said, 'if we could arrange set times for him to work in advance, so that he would never actually be on call. Then he would have less reason to hang around the hospital at other times. He wouldn't have to give any after-care to patients.'

Trying hard to concentrate on what he was saying, Leila stared at him. 'You...you want me to sound him out. Is that it?' she got out, at length.

'Yes, if you would. Then I could make him a formal offer. I'd have to get permission from Administration, but that should be no problem.'

'Why are you doing this when you don't like him?'

'I don't dislike him. The antipathy is on his side,' he said. 'I admire and value his expertise, his experience as a surgeon. I need someone like him.'

For a few more minutes they talked, while Leila felt the clamouring of her heart calm to a more acceptable level. 'I must go,' she said, standing up. It was quite dark outside now. 'I'll get my coat.'

Hers was the only coat left on the bed in the guest bedroom. Clumsily she struggled into it, her mind on what Rupert had said, on her feelings for him.

When she came down he was not in the hall, so she waited for him restlessly until he came from the area of the kitchen, ready to drive her, dressed in a loose-fitting, soft leather jacket.

'Sorry,' he said, coming up to her. 'I just had to make a couple of phone calls to find out what's going on at the hospital. They don't need me.'

His words distracted her, so that she did not flinch away when he put a hand on her face, caressing her cheek, keeping it there. 'Leila,' he said, 'I'm not the swine you seem to think I am. Can't we at least be friends? We work so well together. Don't spoil it by being prickly with me outside work.'

The hand dropped away before she could tell him again not to touch her, then, before she could take evasive action, he leaned forward and kissed her on the mouth, without touching her anywhere else.

It was a soft, lingering, delicate kiss, his lips warm and firm. Involuntarily her eyes closed so that the feel of him dominated her whole being, as though she were rooted to the spot. In that moment she wanted to cry and laugh at the same time with the release of an unbearable tension that had been growing between them all afternoon. That emotion seemed to sizzle between them like a tangible thing…at least, it was there on her side.

When Rupert took a small step forward and took her into his arms, she was incapable of protesting. And she found that she didn't want to protest—this felt as right as anything in her life had ever felt right. In her experience, men often took what they wanted from women. It was not wise to presuppose love, and now she assumed that she was just another pretty young woman that he wanted to kiss, who happened at that moment to be compliant in his arms. Some women took what they wanted, too. She couldn't pretend that women were passive creatures, incapable of their own initiatives. These thoughts flashed through her mind, until she forgot everything but the intense feel of him.

His sigh and involuntary murmur of pleasure as his kiss deepened was Leila's undoing, and her arms moved around his waist as they stood together in the large baronial-sized inner hall. This was the most moving experience that had ever happened to her, she thought wildly as she kissed him back, trembling. So this was what was meant by passion…this all-consuming welter of emotion against which there was no defence.

For long moments they stood as though locked together, until he pulled his head back from her and looked into her eyes, his own eyes dark with a desire that shocked her. As plainly as though he had spoken in precise words, he was telling her that he wanted to make love to her, that he wanted her to spend the night with him, here in this lovely house. And, more alarmingly, she wanted to say yes…yes, please.

Some instinct stopped her. Not yet, she told herself. There was too much baggage in the way. She moved back from him, sliding her arms from around him, although she wanted to take his hand and lead him upstairs to his room, which she could picture in her mind's eye. 'There's a right time and a wrong time,' she whispered.

As he looked at her intently, she felt like falling on her knees and kissing his hand, telling him that she wanted him. Instead, she looked back at him, knowing that her need for him was equally blatant in her expression.

At length he nodded and held out a conciliatory hand to her, which she took. Without another word, he led her to the front door, then in moments they were outside and in his car which was parked in a driveway beside the terraced gardens.

Emotions were so intense that she could think of nothing to say to him on the journey, could not look at him, wanting to weep. If only she could have just taken him, accepted what he had to offer... Neither did he utter a word.

At her house, as she moved to get out, he took her hand and brought it to his lips, kissing first the back of it, then the palm, in an intimate gesture that brought tears to her eyes.

'Thank you for the ride,' she whispered, with her head lowered. 'And for a great afternoon.'

His reply was a squeeze to her hand, then she was out and running up the path. When she was inside with the door closed, she realized that he had made himself very vulnerable to her, had revealed himself to her, in a way that she had not fully reciprocated. He might not love her, but he certainly wanted her...desperately. She sat down heavily in a chair, sobered, not bothering to check the tears that began to fall from her eyes. They were tears of frustration and longing, and of despair because she didn't know what to do.

It was only later that Leila realized she had left her boots at Rupert's house. They were good leather boots, made in Italy, very expensive, otherwise she might just have left them there. Now she would have to get them.

CHAPTER ELEVEN

THE prospect of work on Monday morning, after a restless night, brought a greater than average tension for Leila as she left the house at twenty minutes to seven to drive to the hospital.

Needing someone reliable to talk to, she had more or less made up her mind to take up the offer that Clara had given to her to talk about Rupert. Clara had said, after all, that she, Leila, would be good for him. Now she could use some clarification of that statement, she decided as she manipulated her car along the familiar route. There was so much to do. At some point she had to take her car in for repair, as there were various things wrong with it.

She sighed, contemplating the day ahead, concentrating on the positive. Unlike a lot of people, she was doing a job that she loved. All she had to do was keep on top of it, not let it overwhelm her, take time to smell the roses, as the saying went. Up to now, she had managed to do that quite well. Then there had come the added tension of Rupert Daniels…a pleasant tension some of the time as she longed to see him and work with him, yet love that was not reciprocated, unrequited love, was difficult to bear, so she was discovering anew every day.

By the time she had walked to the locker room at the hospital and changed into her scrub suit, there wasn't much time to spare so, eschewing the delights of the departmental coffee-room, she went straight to the gynaecology unit to prepare for their first case on the operating list in room six.

Rupert operated on Mondays, Wednesdays and Fridays, apart from the times when he had to deal with Caesarean sections and other emergencies. Today she would be the scrub nurse for the first case, as she and Anne had decided on Friday when they had looked at the operating list, then they would alternate with the cases throughout the day.

Anne was the next to arrive. 'Hey!' she said. 'I missed you in the coffee-room.'

As they went about their tasks, they talked briefly about the baptism and the party before Leila went out of the room to the scrub sinks to scrub up for the case.

The anaesthetist was the first doctor to appear, then Greg Amos and Chuck. As Leila bent her head over her task, the tension in her was mounting, waiting for Rupert to come. Would he be any different with her?

While the other doctors were talking to the patient, who was lying on a stretcher outside the room, Rupert came into the scrub sink area, tying a disposable paper mask over his nose and mouth.

'Morning, Leila,' he said, sounding perfectly normal. 'How are you?'

Giving him a quick glance of acknowledgement, she looked down again at her hands and arms that she was soaping, knowing that her eyes had darkened with her awareness of him. 'Pretty good,' she said. 'I left my boots at your house.'

'Oh?' he said. 'You'll have to pick them up some time. Come round for a drink.'

She nodded, not trusting her voice and hoping that he didn't think she had left them there deliberately.

'It's going to be a busy day,' he said, sounding as though they had never stood in each other's arms the previous evening. Perhaps she sounded as nonchalant to him as he did to her. 'When will you have a chance to speak to your father?'

'Later on this week. I'll call my mother tonight to see when he's likely to be at home.'

'That's great.'

In room six, putting on her sterile gown and gloves, she wondered why Rupert was making conciliatory gestures to her father, whom she suspected would jump at the chance to get back into the operating room, if approached in the right way, even as an assistant surgeon where most of the decision-making would be out of his hands.

Trying to tune out the man next to her, Leila focused on their first case, a woman in her late forties who had a large fibroid uterus which had caused a lot of heavy bleeding over quite a long period of time. Now she was to have that uterus removed. Sometimes the uterus could be saved, the fibroids shelled out of the muscle layer of the uterus where they grew, but this time the problem was too severe, and as she would not want any more children she had agreed to the operation. Leila had read the case notes when she had checked the patient.

In the operating room, putting everything else out of her mind, Leila concentrated on setting out her instruments.

In due course, Rupert removed the woman's bulky, fibroid uterus with the minimum amount of blood loss, clamping and cutting carefully, while Leila and the junior surgeons silently admired his skill. It was not easy, as the organ was enlarged and irregular in shape because of the multiple fibroids, benign growths like hard balls protruding beyond its surface. They caused a lot of bleeding because when the woman had a period her uterine muscle could not contract down properly to stop it as normal.

'She'll be better off without this,' Rupert commented as he lifted the severed organ gently through the abdominal incision that he had made and placed it in a bowl that Leila held ready. 'Now we have to make sure there are no bleeders.'

Then he addressed the other two doctors. 'Whatever a woman's age, a hysterectomy is not an operation that she can take lightly,' he said. 'She has to be ready for it psychologically, given enough time to get used to the idea, because having a uterus and ovaries has a lot to do with a woman's sense of identity, her sense of herself as a woman...a feminine woman. So never underestimate the impact of this operation. It is something that should not be undertaken lightly by you, or done unnecessarily.'

Greg and Chuck nodded in agreement.

'I'm not going to remove her ovaries as they are still functional, still producing oestrogens, which she needs, and will be for a few more years. They look perfectly healthy,' he went on.

Later, Leila watched as Rupert meticulously checked to make sure there was no oozing of blood from any blood vessels, that any possible source of a bleed was either sewn up or carefully tied off with catgut or other suture or ligature material.

At last the case was over and the dirty instruments cleared away, just in time for the relief nurse to come in to take over while the nurses went, one at a time, for a fifteen-minute coffee-break.

'You go first, Anne, since you're scrubbing for the next case,' Leila said.

When it was her own turn to go, she saw Clara in the corridor outside the coffee-room. Taking the opportunity, without having too much time to think about it, she approached her.

'Dr Nin, could I...come to talk to you some time soon?' she asked hesitantly, not knowing quite how to couch her request. 'You said I could talk to you...'

'Sure,' Clara said, understanding her immediately. 'If you could come at lunchtime, between half past twelve and one-thirty, I'll have a bit of time then. After that I have an outpatient clinic.'

'Thank you,' Leila said, relieved. 'I'll try to make it.'

Back in the suite, she arranged with the relief nurse to come for the lunch-break between those times.

As she made her way later down to the outpatient department, she was apprehensive about exactly what she was going to say, yet sensed that Clara would make it easy for her. What a peculiar situation this was.

'Come in,' Clara said, closing her office door behind them. 'I assume you've come to talk to me about Rupert, because things are getting a little complicated between you?'

'Yes...something like that,' Leila said apologetically. 'Thank you for seeing me. I don't really know where to start. It's not as though there's anything on his side...'

'Sit down. I can give you about twenty minutes.'

'You said there was something in his past that might...um...prevent him from forming a close relationships, with a woman,' Leila began. 'I'm not saying that he would start a relationship with me, it's just that I want to understand, because I'm...I'm...'

'In love with him?'

'Yes,' Leila said, flushing. 'I know it's stupid when he hasn't really encouraged me.'

'It's not stupid. I've seen how he behaves with you. I'd say he's definitely interested,' Clara said. 'I'm very fond of Rupert, he's like a brother to me. We go back a long way, we've been through some tough times together. I'm not going to be an active match-maker, but I would not be adverse to smoothing the way for him, and you, if I can.'

'I need all the help I can get,' Leila said, smiling.

'So does Rupert,' Clara said. 'I think I know you pretty well, Leila, since we've worked together for a long time, I've seen how you react in an emergency. Most people show their true colours in those times, and their day-to-day integrity…or lack of it. Above all, Rupert needs a woman of integrity. As I said before, I think you would be good for him. I think you would be good for each other.'

Very conscious of time ticking away, Leila told her briefly about her sister, then added, 'Could you tell me about Ashlie Rayburn?'

'Long before your sister came into the picture, Rupert lived with Ashlie for about a year. We were all at medical school together. She was—is—a very beautiful young woman, bright and articulate. She and Rupert spent a lot of time together. It was understood that they would marry. To cut a long story short, and to get to the point, she became pregnant when they were living together, and she had an abortion without telling Rupert that she was pregnant. She should have been more careful. So should he.'

'Oh…'

'Yes, ''Oh'',' Clara said meaningfully. 'Rupert didn't find out until they had a quarrel because she wanted to move out—she had met someone else. I guess Rupert wasn't around enough, he was studying for post-grad exams, and she was working long hours, too, and it all just fell apart. In the course of the quarrel, she told him about the abortion.'

'Not good,' Leila said, the awfulness of it having a profound effect on her.

'Rupert was devastated, for several reasons, as you can imagine. He would have liked a child, but she was not ready, or sure she wanted to be with him permanently. It was the fact that she hadn't told him that was such a shock to him, then the fact that she just went ahead with it without any sort of input from him It's affected his trust in relationships,' Clara went on in a matter-of-fact voice. 'That's been the fall-out for him, whereas for her, she did have a bit of a mental breakdown some time later, which I think may have had something to do with her rather hasty decision. So, you see, it was a bit of a mess all round.'

'And what about now?' Leila ventured. 'Do they see each other?'

'No. That relationship is as dead as the dodo,' Clara said brusquely. 'He's only had casual relationships since then, as far as I can tell. He does confide in me sometimes.'

'Thank you for telling me,' Leila said.

Clara stood up, looking at her wrist-watch. 'I really must go now, unfortunately. What I've told you is in confidence, so I don't want it repeated to anyone else. Not many people know what happened, it was all hush-hush at the time.'

'I won't say anything,' Leila confirmed, saddened by the story. Some things were falling into place now. It was obvious why he had been turned off by Stacey's approach.

'If the need arises, you may tell him that I was the one to tell you the story,' Clara said. 'But, please, choose your moment very carefully, because I value Rupert's friendship.'

'Thank you,' Leila said, her voice a whisper.

'Good luck,' Clara said, holding out her hand to Leila. 'Handle him with care. He's a guy worth having. My advice to you is let him take the initiative. My sense is that if he's really interested he will take it…eventually.'

Chance would be a fine thing, Leila thought wryly as she left the office. In a daze, she made her way back to the operating suite, hardly aware of her surroundings. Not able to face the crowd in the coffee-room, she went to the locker room and quickly ate two sandwiches she had brought with her, and drank from a bottle of water, knowing that if she did not eat she would be hypoglycaemic a little later on.

As she munched, she thought soberly about her emotions. Although Clara had clarified a few things for her, she had also made her own love seem more hopeless. How could she break through that barrier of hurt and mistrust? It must be a big blow to a man to know that the woman he loved and hoped to marry did not want his child. Why, Leila wondered, had she finally told him? To taunt him? That was, in her eyes, unforgivable.

As for herself, the talk with Clara had made her realize more than ever that what she wanted in her life was a fulfilling mutual love. What she actually had now was a one-sided, all-consuming passion that was threatening to take over every aspect of her life, a hopeless passion. If Rupert cared for her, beyond an obvious sexual attraction, he would do something about it, she reasoned.

In the few moments that she had left before returning to work, she called her mother and asked her to sound out her father tactfully with regard to the assistant surgeon job, suggesting to her mother that it would actually serve to ensure that he had a better balance in his life, instead of hanging around the hospital looking for something to do, interfering with the decisions of other doctors. Her mother agreed, saying she would see what she could do.

The afternoon was busy, so that they had just finished

their last scheduled case of the day when the evening nurses came on duty at half past three.

Thankfully Leila took off her mask and paper hat outside the room at the scrub sinks and ran a hand tiredly through her hair. As usual, after a busy day, she felt punch drunk from having to concentrate all day, not being able to relax much on the job.

Rupert came out of the room behind her. 'Leila, when do you want to pick up your boots?' he asked. 'I could bring them to you, or to work, but I think it's more reliable if you get them yourself. I'll be home for sure this evening, after about eight.'

'I...I'll try to get them tonight, then,' she said, hardly able to maintain eye contact with him, as though he would be able to tell somehow that she had talked to Clara about him. 'Shall I call first?'

'No need,' he said. 'I'll be there any way. If you come, you come.' It sounded to her that he didn't care one way or the other.

'All right,' she said.

In the locker room, as she changed, she already felt nervous about going to get the boots, haunted by the memories of being kissed by him.

'Leila,' Anne whispered to her. 'Chuck and I are going out to dinner tonight. You know, I thought it would never happen, I've wanted it for such a long time.'

'He's a great guy,' Leila said sincerely. 'Have fun.'

She dearly wanted to confide in Anne about Rupert, but what was there to tell, really? At the moment she really just wanted to unload her angst as she could not tell anyone about Ashlie Rayburn.

'See you tomorrow,' Anne said. 'Bye.'

'Bye.'

At home Leila made herself a light supper, had a bath

and washed her hair, then dressed in an elegantly casual outfit in muted colours of fine wool trousers and a silk blouse, with a thin, long cashmere cardigan over the top, which came down over her hips and would fit well under her long winter coat. Dressing well did wonders for her confidence, she had always found. Not that she wanted Rupert to think she was making an effort for him. She wore no jewellery, and very little make-up.

At a quarter to eight she set out to drive to Rupert's house, feeling sick with a delicious apprehension. Maybe he would come to the door carrying her boots in a plastic bag and she would simply turn on her heel and go back. Or perhaps he would ask her in for that drink…

It was a cool evening, with a definite hint of frost in the air. Very soon she was going to need those boots.

At a few minutes after eight, she parked outside Rupert's house, relieved to see his car in the driveway yet feeling even more nervous now with the tension of seeing him. This was madness really, this overwhelming, mind-numbing attraction. Over the past few weeks she had come to feel more sympathy for her sister.

The doorbell sounded unusually loud in the silent evening of the exclusive cul-de-sac where few cars went by. As he took his time answering, she felt that she wanted to bolt back down the steps.

CHAPTER TWELVE

AT LAST, Rupert came to the door and swung it right
open. 'Hi, Leila,' he said, 'I was hoping you'd make it.
Come in.' He was wearing black jeans and a dark grey
sweatshirt over a white cotton shirt. To her he looked
unbearably attractive.

As she stepped over the threshold she found that she
was shaking with nerves. 'I can't stay,' she said.

'No, but come in anyway,' he said, drawing her in out
of the cold. 'You're shivering. You can at least get warm.'

'The heater in my car isn't working,' she said, 'among
other things.'

'Let me take your coat,' he said.

'Oh, I can't...'

'At least have a drink,' he said. 'A small one, since
you're driving. I can give you a spot of brandy in hot
water, with honey.'

The prospect of that sounded too wonderful to resist.
'All right. Thank you,' she said, and in moments she had
shrugged out of her coat.

'My housekeeper put your boots away in the cupboard,'
he said, looking around in the bottom of a roomy coat
cupboard in the hall and emerging with her boots. 'I'll
get you some sort of bag to put them in.'

'Thanks.'

Resisting the urge to grab her coat and boots and run
away, she allowed him to lead her into the sitting room—
part of her wanting that more than anything in the world.

If it had not all been so hopeless she would now be happy just to be with him...

A fire was burning in the grate, so she went over to it and stretched out her cold hands. 'This is lovely,' she said. The room was dimly lit by two lamps, cosy, warm and welcoming. Surreptitiously she looked around her, seeing the room anew now that it was not full of people.

'Won't be long. I'll get some hot water to go with the brandy,' he said, 'and root around for a plastic bag.'

The mental image of him, a skilled surgeon, rooting around in a cupboard for a plastic bag made her smile, a gesture to which he responded with a smile of his own that made her heart feel as though it were turning over. While he was away, she tried unsuccessfully to compose herself. The accelerated thudding of her heart dominated her being as she waited for him to come back, wondering what she was going to say to him.

It did not take him long to fix her and himself a drink. 'I've put in a few drops of Grand Marnier,' he said, handing a small mug of tempered glass to her, filled with pale amber liquid. 'It won't impair your judgement.'

'Oh, you guarantee that, do you?' she said, laughing.

'Mmm,' he said, looking at her in such a way that her earlier urge to run away was fast dissipating, although she thought she would stay for as long as it took her to finish the drink.

'Thank you,' she said.

'Sit down by the fire,' he offered.

Obediently she sat stiffly in a wing chair, while he sat opposite her, from where he could look at her without appearing to stare. Exquisitely aware of his scrutiny, she would nonetheless not wish to be anywhere else. Her lips trembled as she sipped at the hot drink, which was sufficiently hot that she would take quite a long time to get through it.

'You know,' he said, 'you seem like a different person outside work. Sophisticated, controlled, elegant.'

She raised her eyebrows at him. 'You've misinterpreted. Certainly not controlled and sophisticated.' The last thing she felt was controlled.

'It seems that way. That's what makes your sense of humour all the more disarming,' he said.

'That's nice. I'm glad you can be disarmed by something, because I'm really a mess of emotional contradictions, and more than a little frightened of you,' she admitted.

'You don't have to be,' he said. 'Why? Because of Stacey?'

'I guess that's it,' she said, wanting to ask him about Ashlie Rayburn, knowing this was not the time.

'Have I ever been mean to you at work?' he said.

'No.'

'You're also very beautiful,' he said softly. 'That's disarming, too.'

'Thank you,' she said, blushing, feeling herself succumbing inevitably to his understated charm. So much for her vow never to get involved with a doctor, particularly an obstetrician...if she could really say that she was 'involved' with Rupert. At that moment she had no real sense of how he felt about her, other than a strong sexual attraction, which she found flattering...dangerously so. There were vibes which seemed to be coming at her with the strength of a gale.

'What are you smiling at?' he said.

'Oh...nothing that I could repeat out loud,' she said.

Rupert talked to her then, as they sipped their drinks,

about gardening, which she loved, about travel, trying to put her at ease.

Although he looked relaxed, she sensed that he was as tense as she was herself.

'You have some intriguing pictures,' she said, when there was a lull in his discourse, looking up at a large painting over the fireplace, which showed flowers in a forest under moonlight.

'I buy work of local, living artists,' he said. 'Anything that appeals to me. Perhaps you would like a tour after your drink. I have so many all around the house that I'm almost out of wall space.'

'I'd like that. My mother's a painter. She paints under her maiden name, and from time to time she has exhibitions,' Leila said. 'She has a small, permanent gallery downtown.' Inexorably, the evening was being prolonged.

'I know,' he said, 'I've seen her work. At some point I hope to buy a painting of hers. She's very talented.'

'I expect she'd be delighted to sell you one.'

By the time they started on the art tour of the ground floor, Leila was warm and even more tensely aware of Rupert, going though the motions with a sense of inevitability. When that was finished they started up the stairs. There were many pictures on the wall beside the sweeping staircase to the upper floor, at which they paused here and there as he pointed out his favourite paintings to her. Watercolours were tastefully interspersed with oils and acrylics.

On the upper landing she paused outside a partially opened door. 'In here?' she asked.

'That's my bedroom,' he said. 'I hesitate to invite you in because I might not be able to keep my hands off you, Leila Hardwick. Would you mind?'

'That's a very awkward question,' she managed to get

out after a moment of hesitation, while her heart pounded. To her horror, she found that she could not prevent a slow smile from breaking out as she looked back at him while he leaned with seeming casualness against the doorframe. 'The point is, do you have any good paintings in there?'

'One or two,' he said.

Stalling for time, she added, 'You mean you could quite easily keep your hands off me out here?'

'It's getting more difficult by the second,' he answered huskily.

As though of its own volition, her hand touched his face briefly, caressingly. Suddenly, everything seemed deadly serious, this moment that could make or break what she most wanted in the world. The contact sent a tingle of shock through her, and she knew that this opportunity was perhaps all that she would have to break the spell of his past. He straightened up, his eyes fixed on hers.

Softly he put a hand on her shoulder, sliding it behind her neck, moving his fingers caressingly into her hair at the back of her head. Leaning forward the short distance between them, he moved his lips over her mouth, tantalizingly, then back again.

The simple, yet shockingly intimate gesture completely disarmed her as she sighed and closed her eyes, putting her hands on his shoulders as he moved close to her and took her in his arms.

His kiss, deep and urgent, blotted everything else from her mind. His hand in her hair held her firmly against him. Letting go of her inhibitions, she put her arms up around his neck, leaning against the firm length of his body. In moments she was matching the urgency of his kisses, completely lost. All the past weeks of waiting went into that kiss.

When Rupert took his mouth from hers and kissed her neck, he was breathing fast. She put her head on his shoulder, eyes closed, clinging to him. More than anything, she wanted to say that she loved him—it dominated her whole being. Instinctively she sensed that it was too soon. I wish I could stay like this for ever, the thought came to her as she relaxed against him and he held her in the protective circle of his arms.

'Leila...darling, will you stay with me? Stay the night with me?' he whispered. 'I want you so much, it's driving me out of my mind. Please, don't say no.'

Not trusting her voice, she moved back from him and took his hand. The naked desire on his face sent a shock of recognition through her and left her in no doubt that his need for her matched her own. Whether he loved her or not was a different story. At that moment she didn't care, as she turned and pushed open the door of his bedroom, leading him inside with her.

'Yes,' she whispered, going into his arms. The room was dimly lit by the emanations of a streetlamp, by which she could see the outline of a large bed in the centre.

'I didn't bring you up here for this,' he said. 'Didn't invite you in for this. But it's what I've wanted for a long time.'

'I want you,' she said softly.

His hands trembled as he undressed her, then himself. There was no reality for her then but the two of them and her passion for him, her love. There were, she assumed, a few very rare moments in life when the essence of everything seemed to come together, when all that was most important was right there within your grasp.

He pulled back the coverings on the bed and swung her up into his arms and put her down on it. Gladly she clung to him as he came to lie above her.

'I haven't...I don't...' she began, wanting to tell him that she had no birth control. Shades of the scenario with Ashlie Rayburn came to her mind, as though the other woman were a pale ghost in the room, standing watching them. At least Ashlie had repudiated him, she would not be a malign presence, a jealous presence. Perhaps he was thinking of her, too.

'It's all right,' he said. 'I have.' She was glad that he was not coy, that he was matter-of-fact. He would not make the same mistake twice. Now she was able to relax, to give in to the moment.

As though to get the presence of the other woman out of her mind, Leila smoothed her hands over his broad shoulders and into his hair, closing her eyes in ecstasy as he moved a hand up over her hip, then over her breasts.

His urgency communicated itself to her and she wrapped her legs around his hips.

'I can't wait.' He groaned the words against her mouth, and she arched her hips against his in acquiescence. As he penetrated her body, she sighed with pleasure, burying her head in the side of his neck so that she would not cry out. 'Oh, Leila...I've wanted you so much.'

Gently he moved in her, bringing the most exquisite sensations that she had ever experienced. 'Rupert...' She whispered his name over and over again, saying silently to herself, I love you, I love you.

In the early hours of the morning they made love again, a prolonged, tender coming together, then at half past five Rupert woke Leila to say he would make coffee and toast for her, that it was time for her to get up if she were to get to work on time.

In a muzzy daze of happiness she dressed and went down to the kitchen, where he stood tousled in a bathrobe, making coffee. They could not stop smiling at each other, or touching.

'Here, drink that,' he said, putting a mug of coffee in front of her. 'I don't want to be responsible for you not being completely compos mentis on the drive home or at work.'

'Thanks.' She was very glad that this was not one of his operating days, as everyone at work would surely see that there was something different between them. As it was, tomorrow would be a strain if she were not to make it obvious to the world of the operating room that they were lovers.

At the door he kissed her goodbye. 'See you at work,' he said. 'Take care.'

As she drove away she was so happy that only a little niggling doubt came to her that he had not said he would see her again in his own time. She vowed to live for the day...one day at a time. Back there she had wanted to ask him about Ashlie Rayburn. The questions had trembled on her lips, but she had not been able to utter them. First of all, she felt guilty about having taken up Clara's offer to talk to her. Rupert might be angry with Clara, and with her, that they had been discussing his very private life. Perhaps one day there would be a right time to ask, perhaps not.

At home she had a quick shower and dressed in work clothes. Somehow she felt different, more alive, more feminine and—whether she was or not—loved. Already she was missing him, as though to be apart was an abnormal condition, so she both dreaded and longed for tomorrow.

On her answering machine there was a message from her father asking her what it was all about that Rupert had suggested he take an assistant surgeon's job. Later on, she

would call him from work, then at some point he and
Rupert would have to get together to talk, if her father
was interested. He did not say categorically that he would
not be.

In a short while she was once again in the car, trying
to shift her mental gears to get into work mode, while her
heart was singing. It would be a strange day.

A senior surgeon was operating that day, a middle-
aged, very pleasant man whose operating time was very
relaxed. It would be a good day, Leila knew as she went
into room six to find Anne already there.

'Hey, Leila,' Anne said, 'I've been bursting to talk to
you. Can we go out for a drink some time soon after
work?'

'Sure.'

'Chuck and I went out to dinner last night. I'm madly
in love, I don't know what to do with myself. And I think
he is, too, although he hasn't said so in so many words.
Neither have I, come to that, although he must know it
by the way I turn into a quivering jelly whenever he gets
close.'

Leila laughed. 'Concentrate on work, then. You get
scrubbed for that marsupialization of Bartholin's cyst and
bring yourself down to earth fast. We'll go out for that
drink tonight.' By that time she herself would have decided whether to tell Anne that she was involved with
Rupert. Anne did not gossip, yet it seemed a little pre-
mature to imply that there was a relationship between herself and Rupert.

'Great,' Anne said, laughing. 'If I do that, then you can
scrub for the cauterization of anal warts.'

'OK,' Leila said airily. 'I'm easy.' It was to be a day
of minor surgery.

At the mid-morning coffee-break she called her father,

pleased to find him at home. 'Hey, Dad,' she said, 'I'm calling to find out if you would be interested in that assistant surgeon job. I think you would enjoy it, because Dr Daniels is a good surgeon himself, and I know he wants you as first choice. If you don't want it, he will have to get on to looking for an alternative.'

'He and I would have a lot to discuss before I would even consider it,' her father said. From his tone, she could tell that he was interested but was trying not to show it too much, and she knew that Rupert would have to get the whole thing OK'd with the hospital administration as her father was over sixty-five.

'Oh, sure, that's understood,' she said.

'Why is he getting you to approach me?'

'He knows you have a certain antipathy to him, I suppose,' she said. 'Shall I suggest to him that he should call you? Or do you want to call him first?'

'Get him to call me some time this week,' her father said. 'I have to sort out my schedule pretty soon.'

'All right, Dad. Must go now, I'm on my coffee-break.'

Smiling to herself, she poured coffee. As far as she could tell, he was hooked. Perhaps, after all, he and Rupert would be good for each other. There was no denying that her father was a superb surgeon, cool and expert in challenging situations, competent in emergencies, which was more than could be said for some of the others. Many times she had seen him operate. It was not surprising that he had been made head of department, had held the position for two terms of five years, because his colleagues in the department had wanted him. Whatever his inadequacies as a husband and father, he could not be faulted in the operating room. She had always felt proud of him there.

Tuesday went by quickly and pleasantly, then on the Wednesday she told Rupert what her father had said.

'I'll call him this morning,' he said, 'get a time set up when we can meet. The sooner we can get it organized, the better. Having your father on the team when needed will ease some of the strain on Chuck and Greg, especially when I have to do emergency C-sections, although I wouldn't call him out after eleven at night. Your mother might have something to say about that, it would be too much like going back to the old way of life.'

'Why are you doing this with my father?' she asked.

'Two reasons. One, I need him, or someone like him, and, two, I don't like to have animosity within the department, even with someone who is essentially retired,' he said. 'A third reason is that I would rather not have a bad relationship with the father of a woman I find very attractive.'

They were standing in the main OR corridor, outside the obs and gynae unit, just before the operating list for the day was about to start. From the way Rupert was looking at her, with what she could only describe as a burning intensity, and because of what he had just said, she felt hot all over. She fervently hoped that when she and he had their face masks in place and the protective plastic goggles over their eyes that they were obliged to wear for surgery, his regard would not be so obvious, or her reaction to it. For once, she was happy about the all-enveloping garb that they had to wear on the job.

'How are you?' he said huskily, after he had stopped talking about her father.

'All right,' she said.

'Will you come out for a drink with me soon?' he said quietly. 'Or dinner?'

Blushing, she nodded, not daring to look around her to

see if others were noting anything different about them. Perhaps she looked cooler than she felt, and they looked as though they were discussing the operating list. Last night she and Anne had been out for a drink, during which time Anne had been so full of her relationship with Chuck that she herself had not had to say much, just listen, and she hadn't got around to talking about Rupert. Now it seemed fitting that she hadn't done so. What there was between herself and Rupert seemed too personal to discuss with anyone yet, although perhaps Clara would be the obvious person if the going became fraught.

'I'd like that,' she said. 'Perhaps a drink.'

'May I call you?'

'Yes.'

With that they parted, and she went to check the first patient of the day. Afterwards, she realized that she had not given him her telephone number. If he was serious, he would get it from her some time.

There was no need to worry, as it turned out, that Rupert would distract her from her work. The day proved to be one of those hectic days, with several major cases, in which a lot of lab work was involved, blood transfusions, getting results from the lab and so on. The anaesthetist wanted blood gases done on his patient quite frequently, so Leila had to take a vial of blood, packed in ice, to the front desk each time, where a porter was organized to take it to the lab, then she had to take down the results when they were telephoned through. It was a day for being completely on the ball.

Neither was Rupert any less than one hundred per cent professional, for which she was very glad, and her respect for him went up a few more notches.

Only when Leila was driving home in the late afternoon did she relax and allow her thoughts to return to Rupert

Daniels the man, rather than the surgeon. What had happened between them such a short time ago came forcefully to the forefront of her mind. Already it was taking on the semblance of a dream, as though she had imagined it all. When something you wanted very much happened, you couldn't somehow believe it, she mused as she tried to concentrate on the road.

It was good to be in the sanctuary of her home, away from the many people she had to deal with as part of the large team in the OR, in spite of the fact that she liked most of the people she worked with and enjoyed being with them. As her adrenaline levels returned to normal, she felt utterly drained.

After a shower she put on a light cotton robe and began to prepare supper, while sipping a glass of ice-cold wine. The ring of the doorbell made her jump. At this time of the day it was probably someone asking for money for a charity, and she was not appropriately dressed to open the door.

Looking through the peephole in the front door, she saw Rupert standing there on her doorstep, and her heart seemed to jump into her throat. Indecisively she stood there, not knowing whether to run upstairs to get dressed or open the door, when the bell pealed again.

'Hi,' she said, as she opened the door, peeping around the edge.

'Hi,' he said. 'I neglected to ask you for your phone number, and since you're not in the book, I thought it best to come here.'

She was immediately struck by how pale and tired he looked.

'I'm on call,' he added, 'so I don't have a great deal of time.'

'Oh... Come in,' she said, nonplussed. 'I'm not actually

dressed. Would you…would you like some supper? I was just getting something ready.' She found herself babbling, unnerved by his presence in her small sitting room, where he seemed to dominate the whole house, very aware as she was that she only had a simple robe on. 'It's just something simple…omelette and salad, crusty bread, and I have some white wine…'

Her voice trailed off as he stood and looked at her intensely, his eyes seeming to burn into hers, his face serious. Then he looked her over, from her damp hair, which she had just washed, down to her bare feet and back again. 'I'd like that very much,' he said, after a moment. 'I wanted so much to see you away from work. I hope you don't mind. I seem to be taking rather a lot for granted.'

'No,' she said, smiling with pleasure at his words. 'I don't mind. I'm glad you came.'

When he came to her she held her breath, as though time had been suspended, and when he took her into his arms she closed her eyes, lifting up her face for his welcome kiss. So this is love, this is passion. The thought came to her before emotion engulfed her like a surge of the ocean.

When they pulled apart he held her at arm's length and looked at her, his face strained and serious. 'Leila, I want you more than I can say. I can't promise you anything, I want to be perfectly honest about that. Right now I don't know what the future holds. I'm a bit of a mixed-up guy with regard to my personal life. But you're the first woman I've met in a long time who seems to have any sort of integrity. Can we spend some time together, see what happens?'

'I…' Tell me about Ashlie, she wanted to say, but the words did not come out.

'Sorry if that sounds blunt,' he said, with a wry smile. 'I guess it's not romantic in the slightest. It's better that way, I think, to be honest right from the outset. At some point I'll tell you about my past, if you want to know. If you don't want me, I prefer that you say so.'

Leila licked her dry lips, wishing she had drunk more of the wine, which might have given her some courage to deal with this situation. It seemed rather as though she was caught between the devil and the deep blue sea, as one of the surgeons at the hospital was fond of saying. At that moment she felt like falling on her knees in front of him, taking his hand, kissing it and telling him that she loved him, that she would take him as he was. Although she knew that the consequences to herself might be dire, that she could be dreadfully hurt if her love were not reciprocated, she knew that she wanted what he had to offer here and now. On that she felt very clear. Better to have loved and lost…and all that.

'Rupert,' she began, her voice barely audible, as she forced herself to meet his eyes, 'I do want you. At the moment I don't care about the future, don't want to think about it. The day may come when I will, but now…' She shrugged.

They were in each other's arms, kissing hungrily, and she felt like laughing and crying at the same time. Mixed in with the exhilaration of her love there was a core of seriousness in her, a sense that this moment was the most important in her life so far, that what she did now would have repercussions throughout the remainder of her life.

CHAPTER THIRTEEN

'WHAT can I do?' Rupert offered as they stood in her kitchen surrounded by the accoutrements of the supper that she had been preparing before he had arrived.

'Well...let me see. I shall enjoy this role reversal,' Leila said, grinning at him somewhat shyly, 'having you as my assistant. You can make the salad, if you like. I've washed all the ingredients, so all you have to do is cut them up and put them in this bowl. I'll make the omelettes.'

As she turned away from him to get eggs out of the refrigerator, he put his arms round her from behind and kissed her neck, sending an acute frisson of awareness through her. 'Don't tempt me,' she said huskily. 'We'd better eat before that mobile phone of yours starts to ring.'

'OK, boss,' he said, releasing her.

Moments before, they had been in her bedroom, making love tenderly, desperately, with a sense of being on borrowed time. Now, as she beat eggs in a bowl, she marvelled at how amazing it was that they each seemed to have exactly what the other wanted in a partner. Never before had she felt so completely at peace, or felt that something was so right with another person.

He was an accomplished lover, making it obvious to her that he had not been celibate since his break-up with Ashlie; he was not like a gauche young medical student who had had only one love. She corrected herself...perhaps only one love, but certainly not one lover. At that moment, she wasn't sure how she felt about it, or about the idea that maybe he was just adding her to a long line of conquests, perhaps in a quest to rid himself of the bitter memories of Ashlie.

In record time, the omelette was ready, the salad made.

'To a long and happy relationship,' Rupert said, raising his glass to her when they were seated at the small dining table in her sitting room.

'I'll drink to that,' she said, smiling, clinking her wine-glass against his.

When they had finished eating and talking about things other than work, while he kept a close eyes on the time, expecting to be called to the hospital, Leila knew that she had to speak now of what was nagging at her.

'Rupert…I was recently in Dr Nin's office in Outpatients and I saw a photograph of you there when you were in medical school,' she said hesitantly, ad-libbing as she went.

'Clara and I were at medical school together,' he said, casually sipping his wine. 'As I expect she told you.'

'Yes. There was a photograph of you and Ashlie Rayburn, so Dr Nin told me about her…in confidence,' Leila said, rushing on. 'Tell me about her, Rupert. I would like to know, because I think that her memory will come between us, like a ghost. If you think it's not my business, just say so.'

If he was angry with her for bringing up the subject, he didn't show it. Only a very slight tension entered the atmosphere. 'My relationship with Ashlie belongs very much to the past,' he said. 'When I think of her, which isn't very often now, I feel nothing but sadness for what might have been and never was. I feel sad for her because, ultimately, I think she suffered more than I did. I think that very soon I won't have any emotion whatsoever in relation to her, not even that small sadness.'

'I see,' Leila said, looking down at the table, twisting her wineglass in her hand, forcing herself to go on. 'Why did Ashlie tell you about the abortion if she didn't want to tell you about the pregnancy?'

For a few moments he was silent, then there was a weariness in his voice when he answered. 'I think she wanted me to hate her, to let her go. At that time she had met somebody else she wanted to be with. Perhaps she wanted to hurt me as well...I don't know.'

'And did you hate her?'

'No.'

'I'm sorry,' Leila said quietly.

'Why should you be sorry?' Rupert said. 'It had nothing to do with you.'

'Sorry for making you talk about it if you didn't want to.'

'I expect it's good for me to talk about it again once in a while,' he said. 'One could say that it was Ashlie's decision, and hers alone, to have the abortion, and in a way I agree with that, as she was the one who would have had to go through the pregnancy and delivery. Somehow, I can't entirely see it that way. I remember how upset my mother was when she lost her baby, going into depression for a long time.'

'Don't tell me, Rupert, if you would rather not,' Leila said.

'I want to,' he said, somewhat brusquely. 'What was devastating for me was that Ashlie totally discounted me, gave me no say whatsoever about the pregnancy. Up to then, I had thought we would marry. I loved her,' he said.

'What if you hadn't loved her?' Leila ventured. 'It might have been the wrong thing to do, to marry.'

'Yes. She didn't love me, obviously,' he said. There was a wry twist to his mouth, although his tone was matter-of-fact. 'For her it was perhaps the right thing, although she had a breakdown later... She's not a hard person.'

Leila gave a tremulous sigh and poured more wine for herself and Rupert. He wanted to talk, and she was willing to listen, eager to understand him.

'I don't think of women as brood mares,' he continued, 'which is something she accused me of, but neither are most decent men indifferent to their own progeny, born or unborn. We should have at least talked about it.'

'I think you should have,' she agreed. 'It's a sad story, and not uncommon, I guess.'

Let him take the initiative, Clara had advised. Up to now she had taken that advice in waiting for him to come to her. There was one thing in which perhaps she could deviate from that. She stood up and looked at her wristwatch. 'It's a miracle that you haven't been called,' she said.

'With Chuck there, I'll only get called if we have to operate,' he said. 'I'm very fortunate with him.'

'Will you come to bed with me again, then?' she asked, holding out her hand to him.

In a moment he was on his feet. 'So soon?' he mocked, grinning, after a few seconds of surprise which quickly turned to an expression of warmth and anticipated pleasure. 'Come here.'

She gave a small scream as he swung her up into his arms and made for the narrow staircase, then laughed and clung to him. 'I wish you didn't have to go,' she said.

'So do I. I'm free this weekend,' he said, with a mock groan, implying that her weight was almost too much for him. 'If you haven't worn me out by then, would you like to spend the weekend with me at my place? We could go out to dinner on Friday evening, then spend the remainder of the time in bed, apart from maybe a walk or two.'

'Yes, please,' she said with a laugh.

Thursday and Friday were very busy days at work, which went by seemingly with great speed.

'I'll pick you up, if you like,' Rupert said to her when they managed to snatch a few moments alone when the operating list ended on Friday. 'About seven o'clock?'

'Great.' She smiled back.

'I've reserved a table for us at a nice eating place I know. Bring some warm clothes, we could go for some long walks through the ravines near my place over the weekend,' he said.

Leila nodded, supremely happy, trying not to show it too much in case he thought she was desperate for a man. Perhaps she was desperate for him, she thought as he walked away from her.

At her home later she packed an overnight bag, got out her warmest winter coat, boots, walking shoes, hat, scarf and gloves. The days were quite cold now, with a definite hint of winter in the air.

True to his word, Rupert was there to pick her up at seven. As she sat next to him in the intimate small restaurant that he had chosen, Leila knew that, whatever the future might hold for them, she would cherish these memories for ever, that she would now live completely in the moment.

They talked about everything under the sun except work as they ate the delicious food and drank wine. In the car afterwards, he turned to her. 'I'm going away, Leila, later on in November, on the 18th, to a professional meeting in Texas. Chuck will be coming with me, so you won't be so busy at work, although the other surgeons might take my operating time, the general surgeons. I'll be away for at least a week, probably more like ten days.'

'I guess some of the other gynaecologists will be going, too,' she said.

'Some of them will. We tend to take turns in going to these meetings, so that the same people aren't holding the fort all the time,' he said, as he started the car.

'I expect I'll miss you at work,' she said truthfully, expressing the thought that came most strongly to her.

'That's what I like to hear,' he said, leaning over to her and kissing her on the mouth. 'I'll miss you. Still want to come to my place?'

Leila nodded. 'Mmm,' she said.

It was cold when they got out at his house, so she put on her heavy coat over her light wool jacket. 'Could we go for a short walk, Rupert? I feel like some fresh air, and I want to walk off some of that wonderful food.'

'Sure,' he said, putting on his own overcoat.

As he took her hand and they began to walk back along quiet streets, under big trees that were now devoid of leaves, where they could see their breath in the slightly frosty air, Leila knew that these moments would be precious to her, too.

'What would you like to do this weekend?' he asked, keeping a firm hold on her gloved hand.

'Oh…walk, talk, sleep, read… Just be with you,' she said.

'It's as good as done,' he said, suddenly putting his arm around her and drawing her against his body as they walked, and she put her arm around his waist.

She wanted to tell him that she loved him, that she was very happy…but she kept it to herself, instinctively.

That night she lay in his arms, with the curtains drawn back in the bedroom so that moonlight streamed in, silvering all that it touched, contrasting with black shadows. Awake, he stroked her hair silently while she placed a hand on his warm, bare chest, feeling the steady beating of his heart.

In the morning he made breakfast for her, bringing it upstairs, where they sat in bed reading newspapers. Then Rupert closed the curtains to shut out the daylight, coming back to her to take her in his arms.

After that weekend they could not get enough of each other. While trying not to make the relationship too obvious at work, they did not particularly try to conceal it either. Leila told Anne some of it, finding relief in conveying her hopes and fears to her friend, who was reliable and discreet. One was always hesitant to disclose an affair with a medical colleague in case it all came crashing down before long and one looked like a fool for having conveyed the message that it might be permanent.

In spare moments at work they talked, smiled, made tentative plans. In their free time they were together as much as possible, spending nights and weekends together.

Work was hectic, particularly in the week before the professional meeting in Texas, as Rupert wanted to operate on patients whom he had on a waiting list of semi-urgent cases. He didn't want to leave anything hanging, as it were. Chuck was busy with him, discharging patients who had recovered from surgery, sorting out all unfinished business. Then it was 18 November and both Chuck and Rupert were gone.

'Feels odd, doesn't it?' Anne said to her that morning as they prepared for the operating list. 'I feel a bit as though my right arm has been cut off.'

Leila nodded. 'I feel like having a good cry myself,' she admitted, having difficulty in coping with the intensity of her feelings, which the absence of Rupert was simply exacerbating, rather than causing. As their relationship had intensified she had found her emotions changing from minute to minute as her need to be with him took on a more and more urgent quality with the passage of time. Sometimes she contemplated her reaction if the relationship should end, if he were the one to end it. More and more, she felt close to tears.

'Perhaps this enforced separation will be good for both of us,' Anne said, giving her a shrewd glance as they went about their work of setting up the room for the first case of the day. 'We're both getting in rather deep. I think Chuck is less complicated than Rupert. Maybe because he's quite a bit younger, he hasn't had time to build up a complicated past.

'Mmm. Oh, Anne, I love him so much, sometimes I feel I'm going mad, not knowing what the future will be,' she said. 'I thought I could live for the moment, but I'm finding it more and more difficult.'

'Sure you are,' Anne said. 'Same here. I think a relationship will be made or broken inside six months, in the sense that you know what you want by then. After that, it's probably good to live with someone for a year or two before you think of making it legal, just to make sure you can live with each other. You don't really know someone until you've lived with them, seen them on a day-to-day basis. People can put on an act when you don't live with them. But it's pretty difficult when you see them day in and day out.'

'I'm nowhere near that stage, Anne,' Leila said, hearing the sadness in her own voice.

'Chuck and I have an understanding,' Anne confided in her. 'We've told each other how we feel—he loves me, and I love him. There's going to be a future for us. He's got to get his post-grad exams in gynae surgery out of the way before we do anything else.'

'I'm happy for you, Anne,' she said.

'Cheer up,' Anne said. 'If Rupert loves you, absence will sure make the heart grow fonder.'

'I don't know if he does love me. He hasn't said so.'

'Have you said so?' Anne asked.

'No.'

'There you are, then. Maybe it's time you declared yourself.'

'It's not as simple as that,' Leila said. 'He has a past. And then there's that business with my sister. I don't want to repeat her behaviour in any way, shape or form.'

'It's time you forgot about her,' Anne said. 'Think about you. You're not like her.'

'I know,' Leila said.

Anne did not know about Ashlie Rayburn. Perhaps it was time for her to tell Anne, get some input from her. But Clara had told her in confidence.

'Chuck's only away for five days,' Anne said, 'thank goodness. I believe Rupert's gone for ten days, yes?'

'He said a week or ten days. He wants to take a few days off while he's there, since it's a long way to go just for a meeting.'

'Chuck doesn't have the money to stay on. The hospital's paying for him to attend the meeting, but not to have a holiday,' Anne said.

CHAPTER FOURTEEN

ON THE sixth day, Chuck was back in the OR coffee-room first thing in the morning, looking considerably more rested than he had when he'd left.

'Hey, Leila,' Chuck said, as she entered the room before going into the OR. 'How are you?'

'Overworked.' She smiled at him. 'Glad to see you back, Chuck. Did you enjoy the break?'

'I did,' he confirmed. 'It was a bit like getting out of prison. Rupert says hi, by the way. And I have other messages that are for your ears only,' he added, his voice low, 'which I'll convey to you later.'

'All right,' she said, laughing.

'Would you like to see a few photographs I took of the hotel and hospital where we had the meetings, plus some of the terrain down there?' Chuck asked enthusiastically.

Leila looked at her watch. 'I'd love to,' she said, 'if I can look at them in no more than three minutes.'

Out of the pocket of his lab coat Chuck took a fat package of photographs and proceeded to take them out and spread them on the coffee-table, while other people milled around to get a look also.

Idly, Leila looked over his shoulder as he bent down and her eyes skimmed over the coloured prints. Then she stiffened, her eyes arrested by a picture of a small group of people. Suddenly she felt slightly sick as she bent closer. In the photograph there were six people, one of whom was Rupert, dressed in casual clothes, his face serious. Standing near him, about two feet away, was a woman whom Leila recognized as Ashlie Rayburn.

The woman looked older, as indeed she was older, than in the picture of her and Rupert in Clara's office, but there was no mistaking her striking dark beauty, the fair skin contrasting with the mass of curly dark hair, the finely etched eyebrows, the large, beautifully shaped, expressive eyes, the wide, attractive mouth.

Leila swallowed and cleared her throat. It did not look as though Rupert and the woman were actually together as they stood too far apart, awkwardly, both with serious expressions, yet Leila felt a sharp stab of alarm and something that she could only interpret as intense jealousy. 'Did you take these pictures, Chuck?' she asked carefully.

'Yeah,' he said. 'I got a bit over-enthusiastic with the camera.'

When the others had lost interest, she leaned forward and placed a finger on the image of Ashlie Rayburn. 'Who's this woman?' she asked, trying to sound casual, though she felt alarm and a sense of betrayal as she began to wonder whether Rupert had gone to the meeting knowing that Ashlie would be there. 'She looks slightly familiar.'

'I think her name's Ashlie something,' Chuck said, rather vaguely, not reacting to the note of hysteria Leila suspected was in her voice. 'She and Rupert were at medical school together, so he said. She's a gynaecological pathologist, which is why she was at the meeting, I guess. She doesn't work in Gresham, otherwise I would have encountered her by now. Maybe she's somewhere in the States.'

'Mmm.'

Not trusting her voice, and not wanting to appear too interested, Leila turned away and poured her coffee down the sink, the prospect of drinking anything bringing a slight feeling of nausea. With her back to the room, she took her time to wash and dry her mug and put it back in the cupboard. After taking a deep, calming breath, she left the room and made her way to the gynae suite.

In a daze, she scarcely saw the people who greeted her, answering them automatically. Again she asked herself the question—had Rupert gone to the meeting knowing Ashlie would be there, or had their being there together been coincidental? She didn't think he would be devious, yet the question nagged at her. No, he was the most up-front man she had ever met. Jealousy was a terrible thing, it did not give you a moment's rest.

At the scrub sinks she saw her father, who had been assisting Rupert for some time now and was also working with other surgeons, having more than proved his worth as an assistant surgeon. In fact, some of the other surgeons were very pleased to have a former head of department assisting them. Leila admired the way Rupert had handled that transition.

'Hello, darling,' he said. 'How are you? I'm helping Dr Carpenter today. Are you going to be the scrub nurse for the first case?'

'Hello, Dad. Great to see you,' Leila said, giving him a hug.

'Hey, careful!' He laughed. 'You'll make me unsterile.'

'You haven't finished scrubbing yet.' She smiled at him. 'Anyway, aren't we always told that you can't sterilize the human skin, you can only make it very clean?'

'In my book, that's sterile,' he said.

It really was good to see him. He seemed to be a changed man these days, with a new lease on life, managing to balance the work he was given with a better home life, spending more time with her mother in mutual social activity. 'Yes, I'm scrubbing for the first case,' she said.

'Great!' her father said. 'This will be the Hardwick team. We'll show them how it should be done, eh?'

'Right, Dad,' she said. Secretly, she wondered how she was going to get through the day when the image of Rupert with Ashlie seemed to be burned into her brain. Rupert had called her three times since he had been away, in the evenings. He certainly had not mentioned seeing Ashlie Rayburn.

The next few days to his return were going to be very long indeed. Although her father must have had a good idea that she and Rupert had a relationship going, he was too tactful in personal family matters to be the first one to say anything to her, although he was not always a tactful man in other regards.

'Your mum and I had a call from Stacey last night,' her father was saying. 'She tells us she's engaged to be married.'

'What?' Leila said, having trouble concentrating, not sure what her father had said.

'Stacey, engaged to be married,' he repeated.

'Are you sure?' Leila said.

'Apparently,' her father said happily, as he soaped his arms vigorously. 'It takes a load off my mind, I can tell you. It's about time she got settled. She said she was going to do everything right this time, hence the engagement.'

'That's really great,' Leila said, at last her thoughts going to her sister, away from her own concerns. 'Who's the man? And when will we get to meet him?'

'Maybe at Christmas. He's a physiotherapist, someone she's worked with for some time,' her father said.

'That's absolutely marvellous.' As Leila began the

scrub process, the thought came to her that the engagement was an indication that Stacey had well and truly got over her former obsession with Rupert. That was one thing to be thankful for. With a sigh, she concentrated on scrubbing her hands and arms.

After her father had gone into room six to put on a sterile gown and gloves, Chuck joined Leila at the scrub sinks. 'Hi, again,' he said. 'One of the messages from Rupert is that he's missing you.'

'Oh?' she said. 'That's nice to know. I guess you didn't know, Chuck, that the woman he was with in the photograph, Ashlie Rayburn, is a former girlfriend of his. I'm telling you that in confidence in case he doesn't want anyone to know.'

'I didn't know,' Chuck said.

'Maybe Rupert is missing me,' she said, recognizing a certain bitterness in her voice, 'but he's also spending time with her, which doesn't exactly inspire me with confidence. How much time did they spend together, Chuck? Tell me that. Sorry to put you on the spot.'

'Well...' Chuck said, his hands under the tap as he began the scrub process, 'we did all go out to dinner a few times. The only times I saw Rupert with Ashlie was when they were part of the small group. We tended to hang out together. Whether he actually took her out, just the two of them, I have no way of knowing. I don't suppose he would want me to say he was missing you if he wasn't.'

Leila sighed. Rupert would not be the first man who was enjoying a sexual relationship with one woman who loved him while still having something going with someone else. Somehow she couldn't bring herself to say that to Chuck, it did not seem appropriate in any way. Although she trusted Rupert, her own lack of confidence, she could see, as well as her jealousy, inspired fear that he did not love her.

'Cheer up,' Chuck said. 'He'll soon be back, and you can ask him yourself. I would, if I were you. Rupert appreciates directness, if nothing else. I got the impression he didn't know she was going to be there, but at these meetings anyone connected with the field can attend.'

'Thanks, Chuck,' she murmured, giving her hands and arms a final rinse before going into the operating room. Enough of all that now. Work was the priority.

Over the next few days Leila was more disturbed than she had thought possible over the photograph of Rupert with Ashlie, even though she conceded over and over again that their meeting had most likely been perfectly innocent, that he had not gone there knowing that his ex-girlfriend would be there, let alone actually to meet her.

Although she told herself this many times, the feelings of anxiety and stress would not be quelled. She loved Rupert completely, had hoped that he loved her. Now she was not sure of anything from his point of view. Logic and probability were swept aside in her sadness at his absence. No one had told her that love could be both joyful and painful to this degree. She did not sleep well, constantly having him on her mind.

On the day before Rupert was due back, Leila had made up her mind about something, which led her in her coffee-break to go to Donna Parsons's office.

'Could I, please, speak to you for a few minutes?' she asked her head nurse, relieved to see her in the glass-fronted cubicle that served as her command post. 'Won't take much time.'

'Sure,' Donna said, shifting her attention from a pile of

papers on the desk in front of her. 'What can I do for you? Come in and have a seat.'

'Thank you.' Leila came in quickly and sat down. 'I was wondering if it would be possible for me to transfer from this OR to the department at University Hospital. For personal reasons...I feel that I would like a change...at least, for a while...' She stopped and swallowed to relieve a tight feeling in her throat.

Donna looked taken aback and took her time in replying, while she considered Leila thoughtfully. 'We have no reciprocal agreement with University Hospital for an exchange of staff,' she said carefully. 'Maybe we should, it seems like a good idea. You would have to apply there in the usual way for a job and resign your position here.'

'Oh...' Leila felt as though she might burst into tears.

'Is it because your father's working in Obs and Gynae now?' the head nurse asked shrewdly.

'Oh, no,' Leila said, thinking that she actually liked working with her father, liked seeing him use his skills, enjoying what he was doing, not trying to take over, to encroach on anyone else's territory. 'He isn't there every day. He keeps a low profile when he is.'

'Rupert Daniels, then?' Donna asked quietly.

'Is it that obvious?' she asked miserably, hanging her head, looking at her clasped hands which she held in her lap, tears pricking her eyes.

'It is to me,' the other woman said. 'Maybe not to all and sundry. We've got eyes in our heads, you know. He looks at you as though he'd like to eat you. He's a very nice guy, so what's going wrong? You may as well tell me if it has come to this. You're one of my best nurses, and I certainly don't want to lose you.'

'I suppose I'm in over my head,' Leila said quietly, cheered slightly by Donna's comments and assuming that she didn't know anything about Rupert's past involvement with Ashlie. 'I care too much. It's painful to be in the same place with him.'

'Because it isn't going anywhere?'

'You could say that…yes,' Leila said, very mindful of the fact, that she had to go back to work in a few minutes. It was good to have a head nurse to whom one could talk, something not particularly common. Donna Parsons, she knew, was divorced and had one child, while rumour had it that she had another man with whom she did not live, so she well understood human relationships.

Donna was silent for a few moments. 'I don't want you to go, Leila, so I suggest that you just back off for a while, let him make the next move—if he is going to. Don't push. I sense with him that would be the wrong thing to do.'

'Yes. It's…just that I can't go on in the same way…'

'You can't *make* things happen where other people are concerned, you can only change what you do yourself. Things will happen, or not happen, in relationships in their own good time. This is the perfect time to start, as he's been away, to back off,' Donna said relentlessly. 'On the other hand, if you really insist on going, I'll see what I can do. I could approach my colleague in charge in the OR at University Hospital, I can't be fairer than that. I suggest you go away and think about it, don't do anything hasty.'

'Thank you,' Leila said, standing up. 'I will think about it some more.'

'My advice to you is be very professional with Dr Daniels while you're at work, which should make things easier here. Then you will just have to be very up-front with him about why you want to back off, without putting

the pressure on him. I'm sure you can do it, Leila,'
Donna said.

Risking being a few minutes late back, she went to the
coffee-room and got herself a cup of coffee, feeling in
dire need of it, and downed it in record time. Then, as
she walked back to her department, she made up her mind
that she would take Donna Parsons's advice. Now that
she had put the possibility into words of giving up her
job, she realized more forcefully how much she loved it
and liked her colleagues.

Both the head nurse and Clara had advised her to let
Rupert take the initiative, she thought soberly, so from
now on she would not be so readily available, so eager to
be with him. Yes, that was it. When she saw him she
would suggest a time apart, if she could bring herself to
do it. Both of them had to be clear on whether Ashlie still
meant anything to him.

With a very determined effort, she put him out of her
mind to concentrate on the operating list ahead of them
with Dr Carpenter, one of the gynaecologists.

In the late afternoon, on the way home from work, she
and Anne went for a drink in a nearby quiet bar, where
they commiserated about work and about their love lives.

'I don't know what to do, Anne,' Leila agonized, with
her hands around a glass of chilled wine.

'You know, sometimes we *think* too much, we don't
do enough. We agonize over what to do, and it paralyses
us.'

'I know…'

'We have to do what feels good and right now, because
what else can we do really?' Anne said. 'I'm making the
most of being with Chuck. In fact, I'm in seventh heaven,

as my mum would say. Every day, every moment is precious. I feel as though I've been handed a wonderful gift.'

'So do I...I don't quite know what to do with it,' Leila said, smiling wryly at her friend across the Formica-topped table. 'Because it's a gift that isn't totally mine, I think.'

Anne paused to take a gulp of lager. 'You can recognize opportunity when you see it. We all have opportunities given to us. And you can't plan to have it all, so I've found. Plans have a way of going awry. As my parents are always telling me, life isn't easy.'

'You're more mature than I am, Anne,' Leila said. 'I hope Chuck realizes what a wonderful woman you are, a rare catch.'

'I'm just a bit more down to earth, that's all,' Anne said. 'I don't think I'm any more mature than you are, I've just had to struggle a bit more. My dad didn't have the money that your family has had, and still has. No private schools, super holidays abroad, university tuition paid for, lots of pocket money and so on when I was growing up. I've had to create my own adventures and opportunities. And another thing I learned is that if you don't ask, you don't get. All things don't come to those who wait.'

'I'm glad you're here, Anne,' Leila said.

'Give him time, and I think he'll realize that he's as nuts about you as you are about him. He's right to get rid of unfinished business first—if there is unfinished business,' Anne said. 'Maybe it really is all over with Ashlie.'

'Maybe,' she said. 'But I don't think he wants to commit himself until he's absolutely ready.'

'Make him realize that he's ready now,' Anne said. 'There are ways and means. And I don't mean anything underhand. Become such a part of his life that he can't let you go.'

'I don't think I know how,' Leila said ruefully.

'Do it subtly, without being possessive,' Anne said. 'You've got it in you, you've got the character and personality for it.'

'Thanks.' Leila laughed. 'I wish I had that confidence.'

'At least you can laugh. That's something.'

On the night of Rupert's return, as Leila was preparing for bed, her telephone rang and the call-display indicated that it was Rupert calling from his home. While her mind raced with wild anticipation, wanting so much to pick up the receiver, she hesitated. So far, she had not decided what she was going to say to him. As much as she longed to be with him, she sensed that it would be better if their first encounter was at work, where she had a better chance of remaining more objective. She had to ask him about Ashlie.

After six rings the telephone went silent, and she stood with her heart beating fast, feeling his presence so strongly as though he were actually in the room with her, her longing for him so powerful that it was like a physical malady. A bitter regret was telling her that sleep was going to be elusive that night.

In the morning, very early, Leila stared at herself in the mirror, her eyes large and haunted, with shadows under them, staring back at her. Today was one of Rupert's operating days. In about two hours from now she would be seeing him.

Once at the hospital, after changing her clothes in the locker room, she avoided the coffee-room and went straight to the gynae suite. It was just after seven o'clock. The operating list would start sharp at eight o'clock, and the first patient of the day would be there, on a stretcher, by half-past seven.

Quickly and efficiently, she began to finish off the preparations for the first case, which the night nurses had begun, then looked out of the door to see if the patient had been brought down yet by a porter from the gynae floor.

No, she was not there yet. But Rupert was...coming down the main corridor towards her, his eyes on her, his white lab coat flapping open as he walked swiftly, with a purposeful air, his face serious. Under the lab coat he had on the usual green scrub suit. Once again she was struck by how attractive he was, and suddenly she felt almost physically sick with anticipation and longing to be hugged by him, kissed...

Unable to move, she waited for him, her mind blank about what she ought to say to him.

'Leila, how are you?' He came up to her, his dark hair uncovered, falling over his forehead, his blue eyes probing hers. 'It's great to see you. I've missed you.' As though on an island of their own, they stood together in the quiet, controlled bustle of staff and patients in the main OR corridor.

Something had happened, she sensed as his eyes searched her face perceptively, and she felt a sharp stab of apprehension. Perhaps, having seen Ashlie again, he realized that he was not over her, that he still cared. The possibility overwhelmed her so that she could hardly speak as she returned his regard. It was so good to see him that she wanted to fling herself into his arms and tell him that she loved him.

'Hello, Rupert,' she whispered. 'I'm all right. How are you?'

'I'm not sure,' he said somewhat grimly, so that she knew something was wrong. 'I just had a talk with Donna

Parsons. She called me into her office and told me that you are thinking about a transfer to another hospital—University Hospital, to be exact. What's wrong, Leila? What's going on?' He pushed the door open wider and moved into the deserted operating room, pulling her with him, letting the heavy door close behind them.

'She had no right to tell you,' Leila protested, a quaver in her voice that she could not control. 'I spoke to her in confidence.'

'She thought you would be angry, but decided that the harmony of her department was more important that your personal sensibilities,' Rupert said as he gripped her upper arms so that she could not move away. 'I've been missing you, wanting to see you. Now I hear that you want to leave.'

She wanted so much for him to kiss her, yet she bit her lip and fastened her line of vision on his broad chest as she decided to plunge right in with what was on her mind. 'I've decided that I would like to back off from you for a while, have a breathing space...' she began falteringly, forcing the words out. 'I thought it might be better if I worked somewhere else. When Chuck came back from the meeting he had a photograph of you and Ashlie. He didn't know what she had meant to you. I saw all the photographs....' At that point, her voice became husky with emotion, and she stopped.

'So that's it,' he said wearily. 'Leila, I didn't know she was going to be at the meeting. I certainly didn't plan to meet her there, although I knew it was a possibility as she's a gynae pathologist.'

'Chuck told me...' she said, her throat painful from tightly held emotion, her eyes aching with unshed tears. So, he had known that seeing Ashlie had been a possibility. 'I don't want to share you with anybody else,

Rupert. I don't want to be a woman who helped you to take your mind off someone else. I thought maybe I could, because I wanted to. But I know now that I can't. I'm sorry.'

'It was just a chance meeting. It means nothing, believe me,' he said. 'I knew before I saw her that it was completely over between us. Seeing her simply confirmed that, so in a way I was glad she was there.' He sounded so reasonable that Leila felt momentarily that she was being ridiculous, but she could not argue with the overwhelming feelings that surged though her.

'Fair enough. I want a breathing space, nonetheless, Rupert. I have to sort myself out. You see, I thought I could be casual, live from day to day, but I find that I can't,' she said, gaining courage as she talked. 'You see...I love you. I tried not to, but it happened anyway. It happened before we became lovers...otherwise I wouldn't have consented.' She laughed apologetically, yet found the courage to say what she had to say. 'I know you didn't want me to fall in love with you, but there isn't anything I can do about it, except remove myself from the scene.'

'Oh, Leila, Leila,' he said softly, still holding her arms, so that it was all she could do not to subside weakly against him. At the same time, she felt like weeping. 'So it's all or nothing that you want?' His face was pale and taut, a certain bitterness in his voice.

'No! No...not that.' Oh, God, she thought as she felt her face crumple with emotion and tears start in her eyes. This was shades of Stacey, the very thing that she had wanted to avoid. 'You see...I thought that I could control my feelings. But I can't. I'm sorry.' That was a massive understatement. She felt that her love, her desire for him had swept her away on the crest of a tide. Love was all-consuming. Well, she had wanted something tempestuous. She remembered saying that to Anne, she thought with sudden wry despair. 'I know this isn't the time or place…'

'Is it marriage that you want?' he persisted, staring down at her fixedly. There was an urgency in his stance, knowing that at any moment some of the other staff might come into the room.

'No! Don't get me wrong,' she pleaded, tears oozing out of her eyes. 'I…don't know what you feel for me, except that you want to make love. Never to be sure of you…I don't think I can live with that. I need time.'

'How much time do you want?' he said.

'Give me two weeks,' she said, dashing the tears away from her eyes, knowing that her explanation sounded confused. With a shaking hand she took a face mask from the pocket of her scrub suit and tied it over her nose and mouth, then she took out her plastic goggles and put them on over her watery eyes. At that moment she wished that Rupert Daniels had never come to work at Gresham General. An innocence, a youthful insouciance was gone from her for ever. Perhaps she had just been forced to grow up.

'And at the end of that?'

'I don't know.'

'All right,' he said. 'But in the meantime, I don't want you to leave here. You're the best nurse I have working with me in this hospital, in any department. The best and the most professional.'

'Um…' She swallowed. 'That's something I'll think about over the next two weeks. Because of what happened with Stacey, I prefer to…to distance myself from you for a while, so that you don't get the wrong impression'

'If that's what you want,' he said, his eyes on her mouth, as though he would kiss her.

'That time will also give you a chance to sort yourself out with regard to Ashlie, in spite of you saying that you don't care any more,' she said, 'because I don't think I could go on if she were in the background any more than she is already.'

'I don't need to do that,' he said firmly. 'I wish I could convince you.'

There was a noise out in the corridor, indicating that their first patient had just been wheeled to a stop outside the door. Rupert's arms dropped to his sides. 'We'll talk, Leila, promise me that. And not at work,' he said, somewhat grimly.

'I promise,' she said, backing away from him. How odd it was that sometimes you were forced into doing the exact opposite of what your body was clamouring for you to do. After his absence, she longed to make physical contact. 'I...I know you said that you couldn't promise me anything, which I accepted at the time, and accept now. It's just that I want to know how you feel about me. I want to know whether everything is on my side, apart from the sexual attraction. I just want to know...'

'It's not that clear-cut,' he said wearily.

With her hand on the doorhandle, ready to jerk it open, Leila turned back to him. 'I was jealous,' she said. 'Pathetic, isn't it?'

Before Rupert could say anything else, she pulled open the door quickly and went out to see the first patient of the day. The porter was still there, and he handed her the patient's case history notes in a folder.

'Morning, Leila,' he said. 'And how are you? This is Mrs Daley.'

'Thanks, Terry. I'm jogging along,' she said. That must be the understatement of the day. 'How are things with you?'

'You wouldn't wanna know,' he said. 'Breathing, any-way. Better than some, that's for sure.'

Leila had to grin, in spite of her preoccupations. 'It's always great to talk to you, Terry,' she said.

'Yeah. See all, hear all and speak all, that's me,' he said. 'See you later.'

Terry was a discreet person, he had to be for the job he did, but there were no flies on him, as the saying went.

'Good morning, Mrs Daley,' she said to their patient. 'I'm the nurse who's going to be in the room with you for your operation, and my name's Leila Hardwick.'

She was going to be all right. Perhaps Rupert thought she was trying to blackmail him emotionally, but she wasn't. Somehow she felt that she was bending over back-wards, to do the opposite.

A moment later, Rupert came out to talk to his patient, his manner calm, giving no indication of the tension that had existed between them.

CHAPTER FIFTEEN

FOR once Leila welcomed 'one of those days', in which there was little time for anything other than the constant rush of work, little to break the sense of concentration. Her coffee-break was five minutes, lunch was a twenty-minute snack.

At the back of her mind, as she did her job methodically and as swiftly as possible, was the realization, as heavy as a sense of mourning, that Rupert had not told her that he loved her. There had been plenty of opportunity during their conversation for him to have done so...if he did. Several times that day she fought down that heavy sense of grief whenever it threatened to overwhelm her. She wished it didn't matter, but it did...it did.

'A good thing we've got strong bladders,' she commented to Anne as they rushed around, clearing up after one patient and preparing for the next.

'Speak for yourself,' Anne said. 'I'm not waiting any longer.'

At last the day was over, their last patient on the operating list wheeled out to the recovery room. Leila removed her paper hat and mask outside of the room, splashed cold water over her face at the scrub sinks, washed her hands. A touch on her shoulder brought her upright sharply. Rupert was standing there, a sheaf of patients' case notes in his arms.

'Leila, I must know,' he said. 'Have you found someone else in my absence?'

'Oh, no...no,' she said.

He nodded, seeming satisfied. 'Will you call me?' he asked.

'Yes.'

That night Leila cried as she lay in bed, wondering if she was doing the right thing, much more disturbed than she had thought possible. In one way it seemed madness to be repudiating the man she loved, whom she wanted more than anything else in the world, whom she longed for with a sharp physical ache. On the other hand, she didn't think she could go on in this casual way when she was consumed with jealousy and all sorts of other emotions, which persisted in spite of his assurances. Time would tell.

In the middle of the night she woke up abruptly, alert, knowing that her brain had been sorting out her dilemmas while she had been asleep, and that now she knew what to do, at least in the very near future. The bedside digital clock said ten minutes past two.

Tomorrow she would call her friend Melanie Harper who worked in the operating room at University Hospital to sound her out about possible jobs there, then ask Melanie to get her an application form from the human resources department if there was anything going. If there was, sad though she would be about it, she would then write out her notice and give it to Donna Parsons. A two-week period of notice was required, although out of courtesy most nurses gave a month's. Leila knew that she could not go on for a month.

Feeling more at ease, she turned on her side and closed her eyes.

When she left the house at half past six in the morning there was frost in the air, a crisp, penetrating coldness that promised winter, and it was not yet light. As she stepped out, she saw something on the doorstep and bent down to pick up a single red rose, its petals rimed slightly by frost. Rupert... His name came to her as she stared at it. Could he have left it there, probably on his way to work, called in early, perhaps, to deliver a baby?

Quickly, with a sense of wonderment, she went back inside and put the rose in a vase of water, a feeling of longing and hope giving a certain comfort. Rupert would not be in the operating room today unless he had an emergency C-section or some other emergency operation to do.

During her coffee-break she put through a call, from a payphone in the front lobby of the building, to University Hospital, to the OR coffee-room there, which had an outside line, having chosen the time carefully when she thought her friend might be taking a break.

'Is Melanie Harper there, by any chance?' she asked the person who picked up the phone. 'This is Leila Hardwick calling from the OR at Gresham General.'

'Just a sec.'

'Hey, Leila!' a voice said, moments later. 'This is Mel. How are you? What's up?'

With few words, Leila outlined her plan quickly.

'As a matter of fact,' Melanie said, 'two girls will be going on maternity leave in a couple of weeks, so maybe you could get in. Mind you, the OR is quite a popular department, but on the other hand, not many people can really do it when it comes to the crunch. So, yeah, I would be happy to get you an application form from Human Resources, and I can put in a word for you with the head nurse if you want me to. She's a nice woman.'

'That would be wonderful, Mel. Thanks.'

'It would be great to have you working here,' Melanie said, 'but I don't suppose they want to let you go there.'

'Could you come round for supper soon, bring the form?' Leila said. 'I'll give a further explanation then.'

'Sure. How about tonight? My cupboard is bare, I know that for a fact.'

''Great! About seven?'

It was all fixed up. With a certain amount of anxiety, yet with a sense that she was doing the right thing, Leila hurried back to her department. As soon as she got the application form for the new job she would write out her notice and leave it on Donna's desk at a time when she was out of her office—a cowardly way of doing it, she knew, but she felt too emotionally fragile to have a confrontation with Donna before her definite intentions were known.

By the Friday of that week her application was in, via Melanie, and her notice letter had been put on Donna's desk just before she, Leila, had gone off duty at half past three. That way, Donna would have the weekend to digest the fact that she was going to lose one of her most experienced and best nurses. Leila felt sad and guilty about that, but she felt there was nothing else she could do.

It was good, she told herself, as she drove away from the hospital, with her emotions churning, to have a free weekend ahead.

On Saturday Leila slept late, and after a shower she dressed casually in some warm leggings and a big loose sweater. As she made herself coffee she felt odd, not spending the weekend with Rupert now that he was back home. It seemed unnatural and she yearned for him.

The doorbell rang as she was sipping her coffee and making herself toast. A sharp premonition told her that it might be Rupert, and her heart leapt, while at the same time she debated not answering the door. No, she couldn't do it.

Yes, he was there, standing on the doorstep, when she looked through the peephole.

'I couldn't stay away,' he said when she opened the door. 'May I come in? We have to talk. I know that's a cliché, but it's the only thing I can think of on the spur of the moment.' His lips twisted with wry humour as he stood there, looking at her. She felt alarmed by how haggard and pale he looked. Had that something to do with her?

She knew that she looked vulnerable herself, her hair damp, her face without make-up, her eyelids swollen from crying last night. Perceptively, his eyes searched her unadorned face.

Silently she nodded, stepping back and pulling the door open so that he could come in, bringing a blast of cold air with him.

'We can't go on like this,' he said, as she closed the door behind him.

'Let me take your coat,' she said.

'Donna Parsons told me you've given in your notice,' he said, shrugging out of his overcoat. 'This is crazy, Leila.'

She took his coat and flung it over the end of a sofa.

'I don't want you to go,' he said, placing his hands on her shoulders.

Leila pressed her lips together so that he could not see them trembling, then, beyond her control, tears started form her eyes and ran down her cheeks.

'Leila, don't cry, for heaven's sake. I can't...' He pulled her into his arms, wrapping her against him, and she sobbed against his chest into the thick wool sweater that he wore.

Then in moments they were kissing frantically, making up for lost time, his hands sliding up under her sweater to caress her bare skin. Helplessly she returned his kisses. Mindlessly.

'I don't know what to do,' she whispered brokenly. 'All I know is that I can't go on like this either…'

'Sweetheart.' He murmured the word against her mouth. 'Don't leave, don't go away from me…please.'

'I…' All she could do was cry, partly from not knowing what to do, partly from relief that he was in her arms.

'Is that a functioning fireplace?' he asked, glancing over to the small fireplace in the sitting room, already piled with scrunched newspaper, kindling and a few small logs. Leila suspected that he was trying to deflect her attention away from her abject misery.

'Yes,' she mumbled, trying to wipe her tears away with the tips of her fingers.

He pulled away from her and, taking a box of matches from the mantlepiece, set about starting a fire. 'It's cold in here,' he said. 'Is there any coffee going? We're going to talk, here and now. It could take some time, so we may as well be comfortable.'

Silently she went out to the kitchen to get them both a mug of coffee, catching sight of herself in a mirror as she did so, noting her blotchy face and red eyes. When she got back Rupert had moved the sofa in front of the fire and was sitting on the floor in front of it, using it to support his back.

'Thanks,' he said, taking the coffee. 'Sit down here with me.'

As she lowered herself down beside him, he put his arm around her shoulders and pulled her against him. 'I want to talk about Ashlie,' he said. 'And about you and me. All right?'

Leila nodded, cupping both her hands around the mug of coffee, leaning her head against his shoulder.

'When you spoke to me the other day about your feelings, I realized more than ever what I guess I already knew—that two people have to talk to each other, be open about what they are feeling, and thinking, as you were,' he said. He paused to kiss her and run his hand through her damp hair. 'Warm enough?'

'Mmm,' she said, not trusting her voice. She listened carefully as he talked about his past, about his lost love.

'I guess we didn't manage to spend enough time with each other, Ashlie and I, once we were both out of medical school,' he said pensively, 'even though we were living together for a while. What that experience—the breakup and what led up to it—did for me was make me realize how quickly, and with what apparent ease on her part, something that I thought was good and solid could be dissolved. It wasn't my choice. The shock of it was devastating.'

'Go on,' she prompted.

Rupert sighed, leaning back against the sofa, closing his eyes. 'I guess I grew up, fast,' he said. 'Since then, my views on marriage have been that I would rather not get married unless I could be as certain as anyone can be that it would be permanent, that I wouldn't bring children into the world unless it could be permanent. You see, I don't see any point in marriage unless it's going to be for good...that's the whole point of it. It's easy to have a wedding ceremony, a big party, but do you have the maturity to stick with the relationship through better or worse? That's the question that has to be asked.'

'I agree with all that,' she said softly, looking up at him, 'but why are you saying all this to me, Rupert?'

'I've seen too many awful scenarios in the work that I

do,' he went on. 'I've seen children from horrendous backgrounds, because their parents are basically children themselves in adult bodies, immature, narcissistic, self-absorbed and self-centred. To be a good parent you have to be centred on your children to a large extent, to be constantly sensitive to their needs, which entails putting your own ego on hold for a while…often years. There are some people who couldn't put their ego on hold for five minutes. If you can't hack it, don't get into it.'

Leila took a swallow of coffee and stared into the fire, feeling calmer, more at peace. 'But there must be a lot of people who think their relationship will be permanent, then it isn't,' she ventured.

'It helps to be mature, to have reached a certain age,' he said.

'You can do the opposite, let it go for too long,' she suggested, 'then you lose the courage to make that leap of faith—which I think getting married is, to a large extent. And you lose that certain optimism of youth. You could say that the same applies to both getting married and having a baby. You know, "To everything there is a season". I sometimes think that anyway.' The words had just come out. She hadn't realized that she thought like that. 'Perhaps you get too used to being a single entity, not able to adapt to another person in a close relationship. You know, if we wait for the perfect time for something—the perfect time to have a child, for instance—that time may never come, because we can always think of a reason not to do something, at least one reason.'

'A leap of faith,' he murmured, stroking her hair. 'Yes, I guess you could call it that.'

'Based on common sense and love, of course,' she qualified, gaining courage. 'A leap of faith is not a leap into the dark.'

When she looked up at him he smiled down at her, then kissed her gently. 'Don't go away from me,' he said again, softly.

'Why should I not?' she said, very seriously.

Rupert put a hand on the side of her face and turned her towards him as he looked down at her. 'Because I love you,' he said, brushing his lips against hers. 'I love you to distraction.' When they kissed, long and lingeringly, tears fell from her eyes again which she could no more control than the beating of her heart.

'I love you so much that I don't know what to do with myself. I think I'm going mad. Do you really love me?'

'Let me show you,' he said, smiling, nuzzling her neck, kissing her eyelids.

'Oh, Rupert...' she whispered, smiling back at him, touching his face tentatively, hardly able to believe what he had said, because it was something she wanted so much. It seemed like something in a dream. 'What am I going to do?'

'Stay with me,' he murmured. 'That's what you can do.'

'Can you put your past behind you, so that it isn't intruding?'

'Yes. It's you I love. When Donna told me you wanted to leave, that was instantly confirmed. It was something I'd known for some time.' he said. 'You fill my life.'

'But you didn't tell me,' she whispered.

'I believe in taking things slowly, and I wasn't sure that you would want me. Love means commitment, it means marriage...eventually,' he said. 'I knew the last thing you wanted was to be married to an obs and gynae man like your father.'

'I'm so mixed up,' she confessed, sniffing. 'All I know is that I love you.'

Rupert stood up, then pulled her up into his arms. 'I want you to know that I'm not like your father, never will be. We're very far apart, and not just because he's of a different generation. He's a good man, a good doctor and surgeon, who doesn't know how to balance work with other aspects of life.'

With her head against his chest, her arms around him, Leila felt the deep contentment of love creeping over her. What he seemed to be saying was that he wanted to be with her for always, and she closed her eyes, revelling in the moment, the feel of him against her.

'Will you marry me?' he asked huskily. 'You are everything that I want. For my part, I will do my utmost not to be the stereotypical workaholic obstetrician that I know you've always dreaded.'

'I'll think about it,' she teased, smiling up at him. 'Show me how much you love me first.'

'Better think fast,' he said, kissing her. 'I can't wait much longer.'

As they lay in her bed, twined in each other's arms, he said, 'I want to stay here all day and all night.'

'All right,' she agreed.

'Have you thought yet, Ms Hardwick?' he said, teasing her, propped up on one elbow, looking down at her.

'Rupert, I love you so much,' she whispered. 'In spite of my best intentions, here I am with an obs and gynae man.'

'They're the best kind.' He grinned at her. 'We'll make that leap of faith together.'

'And as I said once before…yes…yes, please,' Leila said.